MURDER
IN THE
MAPLE WOODS

Can a Riddle Be Solved in the
Remote Sugar Camps of Maine?

CLAIRE ACKROYD

Designed and produced by:
Maine Authors Publishing
12 High Street, Thomaston, Maine
www.maineauthorspublishing.com

Printed in the United States of America

This book is dedicated to the *acericulteurs* in Somerset County, and to pit bulls and their rescuers everywhere.

In the presence of nature a wild delight runs through the man in spite of real sorrows. In the woods we return to reason and faith. There I feel that nothing can befall me in life, no disgrace no calamity which nature cannot repair.

RALPH WALDO EMERSON

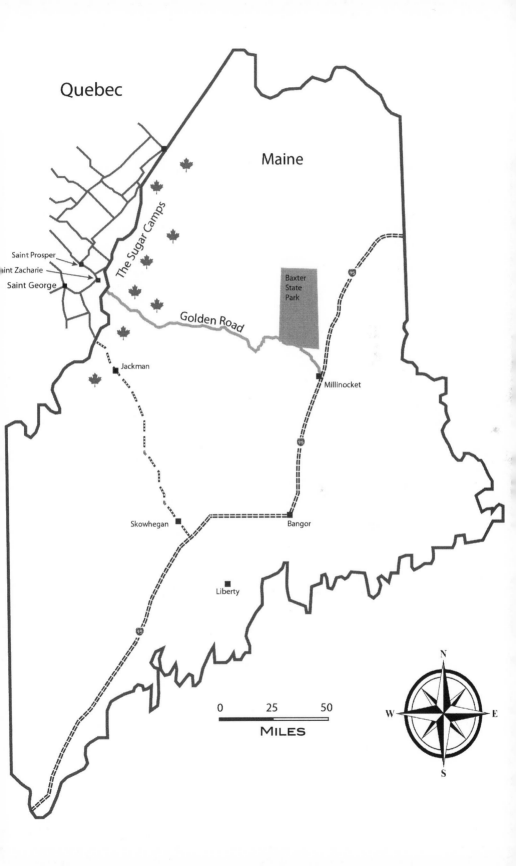

Quebec

Maine

The Sugar Camps

Saint Prosper
Saint Zacharie
Saint George

Baxter
State
Park

Golden Road

Jackman

Millinocket

95

95

Skowhegan

Bangor

Liberty

95

| 0 | 25 | 50 |

MILES

N

W   E

S

1

Simone Thibodeau threw her snowshoes into the back of the truck, reached for a nut bar from her stash in an old milk crate, and tried to close the tailgate without transferring a layer of wet mud to her work clothes. The attempt failed. Fuck it, she told herself. Enough for one day. An hour and a half slogging through deep, sticky April snow, ducking under sap lines and sliding down snow banks, and she had had enough. She hauled herself into the cab and took out her work log. One more maple sugar camp inspected, one more industrious *acericulteur* reassured that she had found nothing to report that could mean his syrup would not qualify as Certified Organic, one more hard day on bad logging roads, struggling to communicate in the slightly shaky French she had learned as a child and largely forgotten until a few years ago.

Her co-worker had already fully occupied the passenger seat and was poking and swiping at his smartphone. There's no signal here, fool, she wanted to say, but preferred to keep him silent and at arm's length, communication-wise and physically. She had written him off as a dolt three days ago when they had started this year's round of remote sugar camp inspections along the northwestern edge of Maine, but she was doomed to spend another forty-eight hours with him and silence was her best defense against killing him or just abandoning him at the end of a long, untraveled road. Besides, if she was going to get paid for her work, his contribution was needed.

"Find anything there?" she asked him reluctantly as she shoved files, a calculator, and the tree diameter tape from her pocket into the old briefcase that lived behind her seat. Before they left the camp, she needed to at least confirm that his part of the job, inspecting the sugar camp itself with its complicated equipment and record-keeping needs, had not revealed any serious problems.

"Nah. Just like you said, no issues. They made two barrels yesterday but sap is hardly flowing. Sucky season," he offered.

OK—so that meant they could head back. Simone clicked the 4-Low switch by her knee and put the truck into gear. The front wheels had sunk into a wet pile of snow as they'd arrived and it would take the truck's best moves to get them back onto the camp drive. Driving under these conditions sucked. The roads had deteriorated since they'd started out that morning. Unseasonably cold weather over the past few days had meant frozen dirt roads and easy traveling, but now, rising temperatures and a weak afternoon sun had thawed the surface and turned the camp road into a greasy mix of mud and slush. Fishtailing out of the camp's front yard, she made it to the top of the slope that led down to the Golden Road—the ninety-mile logging highway that bisects Maine, from Millinocket to the Canadian border, crossing at Saint-Zacharie.

Once on the comparatively solid ground of the Golden Road she put the truck into 4-High and headed due west to the border. Six miles passed, and glancing at the now comatose burden beside her, she pulled into a camp decorated with red plywood maple leaves and a sign that read *Thibodeau et fils, Érablière* with a familiar logo that announced "Certified Organic by Maine Organic Maple Producers." She beeped a couple of notes on the horn and a disheveled head under a moth-eaten wool hat poked itself out of the camp door.

Her uncle slithered over the ice and leaned into the truck.

"*Salut, mon oncle,*" she greeted the face under the hat. "*Ça coule?*" Sap had not been running in the cold weather, but her uncle's camp sat in a protected fold in the ridge that supported these miles of sugar maples, and the milder afternoon might have brought hope to his favored spot.

"*Oh,'tsit peut,'tsit peut.*" He moved thumb and forefinger an inch apart to indicate the poor performance of his sugar bush. "*Demain, peut être,*" he added, always the optimist.

"Hope so," Simone replied, too tired to wrestle with French and in the full knowledge that her uncle's English was well up to the task of talking to her. The temptation to stay and chat lost out to the desire to get out of heavy clothes and into a hot shower at the cozy *gîte* in Saint-Georges, across the border in Canada and still most of an hour's drive away. Sugar camp inspections came with complicated logistics. The Maine side of the border was where the work was, but the unpeopled woods provided no accommodations for inspectors. The nearest bed and breakfasts were on the Canadian side, where small towns nestled up against the US border and their source of revenue.

"Gotta go—thought I'd just say 'Hi.' Gotta get Sleeping Beauty here back to his supper." She nodded at the lump in the passenger seat and rubbed her uncle's hat.

"See you soon," she assured him as the truck rolled sideways down his drive and straightened out on the hard road at the bottom.

The trailer that served as the Canadian border post was quiet. Logging traffic was slow now that the roads were turning sloppy, and the young guy who manned the station did not look up from his computer until the two inspectors walked in, guiltily eyeing their boots and the sign taped to the wall that loudly requested No Mud on the Floor Please. In a concession to the inevitability of mud-caked users of the office, the linoleum floor at the entrance had been replaced by an open, ferociously coarse-toothed metal grid laid over a pit cut into the floor.

Moving carefully so as not to dislodge clods of dirt and ice once she passed the gridded mud trap, Simone reached the wall phone that connected to a mysteriously friendly official in some distant headquarters, who recorded the information off her PPTRA card, the recently invented layer of bureaucratic effort to keep tabs on anyone moving in and out of Canada through these remote crossings. The lump's turn came next, and she heard him declare "Julian Danforth," his birth date, and his card number. Barely taking his eyes off his screen, the guy waved them on with the redundant exhortation to "drive safe."

The long road through the small Canadian towns that lie along the border with Maine was reasonably clear. Back in Saint-Georges, food and a beer were the first order of business, followed by tedious paperwork demands. It was past ten when Simone thankfully hit Send on the last report to MOMP and headed for bed. Two more days to go and she could look forward to a paycheck and some spring skiing.

She set her alarm for an early wake-up, giving herself time to return a call that had come in during the day from the MOMP office.

Communicating with the mother ship was never easy in this situation. Everyone recognized that in the maple camps, phone contact was poor and Wi-Fi worse, so business had to be taken care of before they set out. The strange geography of the job was part of its appeal.

She had stopped trying to explain it to the flatlanders in the civilized southern end of Maine. Most Mainers, even those who professed to be backwoods aficionados, lacked an understanding of this part of the state, with its big sugar camps operated largely by French-Canadians. They have no idea what goes on up here, she reflected with some satisfaction. The north Maine woods were just groomed ski trails and easy-access summer camps to them, and they rarely made it this far from home. As the old Mainers love to say, you can't get there from here—not in winter, anyway. Once past Millinocket there are no towns, only scattered hunting lodges and campsites. She had read an account of a daring duo who had driven the length of the Golden Road one summer, depicting it as a life-in-your-hands plunge into the great unknown. True, in a way, she thought, and long may that idea hold.

* * *

It was barely light the next morning as Simone eyed her sidekick—nominally her superior, as on-staff inspector at Maine Organic Maple Producers, rather than a freelance contractor as she was. He was tucking in to a second round of toast and blueberry jam, topping off the substantial plate of eggs and ham supplied by the solicitous proprietress of *La Gîte des Érables*. Leaving him to it, she went out to check temperatures and return the call from the MOMP office.

Should be that dumb-ass they call, she thought, as she hit the Call Back button. How come they bother me when he is their boy, she asked herself? Whatever. She liked Linda, the efficient and usually supportive chief cook and bottle washer at MOMP. Getting through to her, she apologized for ignoring her call from the day before.

"No sweat," came Linda's customarily unruffled reply. "Had a favor to ask. Wondered if you could take a quick look at the LePage camp on the Golden Road. We got a tip that something is up. They may not even be operating, but they did send in an update, so we're trying to figure if we

4

should schedule them in for the next run. We've tried to reach them by phone but you know how that goes."

Conflict of interest rules meant that Simone could inspect neither her uncle's camp nor that of his immediate neighbor the LePages, whom Simone had known since her childhood and about whom she had definite opinions.

"Okay, I'll see what my uncle knows, if you like. Not much gets by him, and he's got Mattie, his weird grandson, up there helping him this year. A mouse wouldn't fart on the Golden Road without Mattie writing it down and investigating it."

"Thanks. Appreciate it. If something looks sketchy we'll give Robert a heads-up, and backup if it comes to that." Robert was the mop-up guy, scheduled to finish the few inspections that would linger after Simone and the dead weight had completed the lion's share of the project. He was a relatively inexperienced inspector and would be given some strengthening help if needed.

"Don't do anything that could get anyone into trouble," Linda cautioned. "Just let us know if they look like they are operating. The tip we got could just be crazy Frenchmen out to sabotage each other."

"Easy on the crazy French," Simone said. "That's my people you are blaspheming. I know they are crazy but *you* don't get to say so."

"Hey, no offense. But they've got to be crazy to work that hard in this crap climate."

Linda's open-minded view was that anyone working in organic food production was half nuts and half ideologue, herself included. The population of backwoods maple producers from *La Beauce* added to the diversity of the situation without in any way reducing the level of crazy.

Passing through the American customs checkpoint in Saint-Zacharie an hour later, Simone made her usual request to use the spotless bathroom just behind the office. The nice American Border Patrol guy who checked papers and gave them the maple camps' activity report for the day was used to her need for a pee, one hour after three cups of coffee. Ignoring the request on the wall to *SVP, Faites Partir le Fan*—presumably directed at bathroom-users with more than a bladder-full to take care of—she emerged to find Julian in line behind her. Cool, she thought, he'll be in there for a while, since he never hurries at anything. I get a few minutes to chat up the cute agent.

"Any of the LePage tribe been in?" she asked casually, avoiding eye contact lest her interest in the guy be detected. He had started at the post recently, replacing the grumpy little man who had given them a hard time for years, taking ages to check paperwork and asking stupid questions about fruit. (Seriously, she had wondered, do I have to declare my lunchtime banana? I will eat the damn thing right here if I have to but I will not be accused of smuggling bananas. She had lied instead, which seemed the easiest way of dealing with the pinhead.)

"LePages? They're in there, I think. I don't see them crossing that often. Your aunt went in earlier this morning. Said her guys needed clean underwear and food. She thinks they'll be busy later—looks like a good sap day coming up."

His name, right over his right breast pocket, was Haskell. Definitely a Mainer. Handsome, too. He has nice hands, she thought, as he handed her back her passport. Wonder where he lives when he is not manning this forsaken outpost. And whether he has a first name. Looks like a Ken or a Jim.

To her surprise and discomfort, Haskell seemed to be in a conversational mood.

"So, how come you have an American passport and a Canadian uncle?" he asked her, apparently unaware of any impropriety in interrogating a border-crosser whose paperwork left no room for suspicion.

"Easy. My dad made the switch before I was born. He was a university guy in Orono. Uncle Serge is the true-to-his-roots one. Never could get him out of Saint-Prosper."

"What about you?" Haskell asked, venturing further into unregulated territory.

"Me? Confused, I guess. I'm a university brat who would rather be kicking around the woods. That's why I do this job. Gets me up here and I get paid for it."

Julian emerged from the bathroom, buttoning and adjusting, the fan roaring behind him. Simone managed a raised eyebrow glance at Haskell, who twitched his nose just enough for them to register shared disgust and amusement. As she gathered her papers and headed for the door, he caught her eye again.

"We're still closing early—winter hours till the end of the week," he warned. The border crossing's hours were altered to accommodate logging traffic, and sugar camp operators and inspectors had to adjust their schedules accordingly. When roads were frozen and logging trucks able to use them, the border stayed open all night for truckers to take advantage of the coldest hours, closing by day as early as 2 p.m. so border agents could get some sleep. Once the roads softened, heavy trucks were banned and regular summer hours were resumed. Haskell had evidently got the same weather report as her uncle: warming days that predicted good sap flow and sloppy, treacherous road conditions. Two more days and logging activity would have to stop for the season.

"Thanks for the heads up. We'd better get going. We should be done by 2. We've got three to do here today, then a bunch on the Baker Road tomorrow."

The Baker Road, accessed through the crossing at Sainte-Aurelie, a few miles farther north, had more sugar camps than the Golden Road. Four were still to do, the last on Simone and Julian's schedule before their assignment was complete.

"Okay, take care then. Camp roads may get real bad. The Poiriers are using their big truck to get in and out now." Haskell seemed extra solicitous, Simone thought. Better not assume I can't drive anywhere some damn Poirier boy can drive, she thought to herself. And in a sensible-size vehicle too. Those fools just like an excuse to slam that huge truck into snowbanks and spray mud all over the place. Little bit of finesse and a good low gear and I can get this truck anywhere those assholes can go.

"We'll be fine," she assured him as she prodded Julian down the steps and into the reliable little Toyota.

"Catch you later," she ventured, hoping it didn't sound too much like an expectation.

* * *

Heading once more down the Golden Road, Simone shoved the Hannaford's supermarket bag full of the day's files toward Julian. Make him do his job, she thought.

"Three easy ones, right boss?" she asked, hoping that he would not notice the sarcasm she was unable to leave out of her voice. This dope had been foisted onto her via MOMP's board of trustees, well-meaning but frustratingly unaware individuals who thought that an idiot nephew with a trendy new degree in some sort of sustainability from one of those fancy-ass private colleges was just what this off-the-grid project could use. Simone had little time for the spoilt offspring of wealthy city folk. Some of them turned out okay—a bunch had moved into the state in recent years, taking on run-out farms and changing the face of agriculture in Maine, but in her view, this doofus was the other kind, a lazy dope with a sense of entitlement and a family with enough pull to get him a job with MOMP. Oh well, thought Simone, job security for me. As long as he is around they will need me to make him look useful. She couldn't help recollecting how much more fun it had been the previous year, when she had come up with Andy, a seasoned inspector and hard-working farmer in his other life. They tore through the work, collaborating efficiently and laughing at the obstacles they had encountered. One camp had a creepy guy, a weirdo with a pervy grin who had tried to get Simone to see his pump station with him. "Ask him to show you his pump" had become the joke of the trip.

"Right, two Bolducs and the Morissette place." Julian was waking up and pulling files out of the bag. The Bolduc family had a significant presence in the small, closed world of these camps. The senior Bolduc, an energetic man in his late sixties, had initiated the contact with MOMP, figuring out the possibility that the growing demand in the American market for organic foods could benefit the maple business. Maple syrup was a natural candidate for organic certification, he had explained to his skeptical co-producers. You had to go out of your way to make it non-organic, and there was a small but useful premium paid by the big buyers for certified syrup. Furthermore, this group of producers was operating within America, able to bypass the FPAQ, the Quebecois cooperative that controls the flow of Canadian syrup into the market. Nonetheless, the prospect of paperwork and burdensome inspections had been sources of resistance, which he had overcome in part by forming his own cooperative among this group of Maine producers, providing them with binders of ready-made forms and boxes of standardized barrel labels to take the sting out of record-keeping. The few holdouts, who resented the significant charge he levied for these services, were a pain to the inspectors, who had come to rely on the co-op's organized records. The three camps on the day's schedule were co-op operations, run by various off-shoots of the Bolduc family and the charming Morissettes. No problems anticipated.

"Okay. So how about I do the woods for the next two?" Simone suggested. Sugar camp inspections were done in two parts. The first was the sugar house itself, a complex setup of holding tanks, the costly reverse-osmosis systems that concentrate the sap prior to boiling, the big boilers that look for all the world like huge locomotives out of the steam era, and the final filtration in which finished syrup is mixed with diatomaceous earth powder and then pushed through paper or cloth filters that remove the powder and any lingering impurities. Included in the camp inspection was the record keeping needed to verify the purity of the finished product and to make it possible to track every finished barrel back to its production day. Simone preferred the other part of the job, touring the woods and remote pump stations, inspecting the sap lines and checking that tapping standards were being met. Canadian organic standards allowed trees with a diameter, measured at breast height, as small as eight inches to be tapped, in contrast to the ten inches demanded by American standards, and it was not uncommon to find taps in small trees along the more distant lines. She rather enjoyed encountering these. Her discoveries were usually met with hung heads and blame placed on hired tapping-season workers who seemed to be confused about which side of the border they were working on. She did not anticipate any such problems here. The Bolduc family ran a careful operation, and she knew the younger Bolduc boys—large, friendly young men with a feel for speed and nice powerful machines at their disposal with which to express it. A run up through their sugar bush would help to clear the cobwebs out of her mind. She didn't feel like last night's sleep had been enough, but if you didn't get the reports done the same day, the job became a nightmare and no amount of notes could solve the challenge of remembering which fuck-up had been found at which camp.

The Bolducs' trees, a sweet long stand of healthy sugar maples, ran along the same ridge as her uncle's. What had been two separate operations had been combined under one name, the two sets of cousins who had inherited their parents' businesses finding efficiency and economy in working together. So while Julian still had two camps to inspect, the trees and distant pump stations could all be seen in one long cruise through their woods. With the prospect of following well-packed trails that snaked along the sap lines and provided access to the pump houses, Simone was prepared to make this a thorough inspection of the farthest reaches of the extended territory.

They were greeted by a collection of the Bolduc boys. Pierre, the tallest and youngest, was assigned to Simone, and had two work-horse snowmobiles waiting for them. She fired one up and followed her bulky snow-suited guide. Cruising up along their main lines took them to the top of the ridge. Undoing the bungee that held her snowshoes on the rack on the snow machine, Simone set off on a mission to find anomalies in the tapping maps and errors in the size of trees tapped, a task made easier in this case by neat plastic cards at the top of each line, the line number and tap count clearly marked on each one. The snow was deep, which made the going slow. She floundered her way down a slope, ducking under lines and fouling her snowshoes in the puckerbrush, but could find nothing to report on. The correct micro-taps, lines in good order, small trees left untapped to grow, anchor lines holding up the tubing, and gear all installed without putting nails in trees. She lingered longer than a quick check demanded, announcing to the patient Bolduc boy that MOMP was requiring closer inspection this year of line-anchoring and tensioning systems. The design of the tubing to carry sap from the trees is as much art as science. Main lines need the correct slope for efficient sap flow and are run though maple stands to allow the feeder tubing to connect to as many trees as possible. The process starts with the installation of taut wires to which the vacuum and sap lines are attached. Anchoring systems at the ends of the lines and tensioning wires that hold lines level as they snake through maple stands carry potential for significant harm to the trees, and inspections now were paying closer attention to this matter.

Using this as an excuse, and knowing that Julian would take far longer than needed to check records and the two sugar houses, she followed a main line for a while, noting careful attempts to pad wires that circled trees, and to use anything but maples to anchor the lines. She liked being up there in the distant woods, away from the noisy camps. She felt like she knew who she was there, unchallenged by the impossibility of dealing with people and their expectations.

"Trees look good," she commented. "Serge says the season sucks, though. I think he's wondering why he's bothering. Not sure the LePage camp is even operating." She dropped the thought casually, wondering if the Bolduc boys would let anything useful slip. It produced a French expletive from her guide.

"*Ces trous de cul.*" Clearly no love lost between the Bolduc clan and the LePages. "They were in when we were tapping earlier, so I guess they are working. They never talk to anyone.

"Season's not over," he added. "Next few days look good. Maybe we'll all get busy."

From the trees, they moved down to the pump stations at the foot of the ridge. Sap was beginning to run. The pumps running the vacuum on the lines were operating noisily and the big stainless collection tanks were starting to fill. Simone's checklist recorded adherence to the rules: everything clean, contained, and free from contamination.

Having failed to find anything wrong at either Bolduc camp—nothing to report apart from two high-tech operations that combined over 90,000 taps between them, both struggling like everyone else with a slow, cold season—the two inspectors moved on to the Morissette camp at the end of a long, bumpy access road.

"My turn for the woods," Julian declared as they climbed out of the truck. Neither of the Morissettes spoke functional English, and Julian had been forced to admit that a few years of prep school French and a summer with a vineyard-owning family in the Loire valley had not prepared him for the Beauceron dialect, with its skipped consonants, pinched vowels, and strange guttural sounds. It was therefore Simone's pleasant task to check that camp and records were in order, and to accept a cup of camp coffee while the Morissettes fussed over her.

"Fine by me. Have fun." Simone was pleased to see him plod off on his snowshoes to the one pump station, within sight of the main camp. The Morissette operation, a small, older camp run by the couple as a winter retreat, was an easy one to inspect. They still used the original log cabin, which was tricked out by Mme Morissette in gingham curtains and table cloths—a cozy little home in stark contrast to the utilitarian work camps that were the norm at the larger businesses. Mme Morissette kept a neat set of books and a daily work journal, and Simone's check of the camp was done before Julian came sweating out of the woods.

They were back on the Golden Road by 1 p.m.—time to spare even if the border closed at 2. Simone reminded Julian that Linda had asked them to look over the old LePage camp. She got a "whatever" grunt in reply. The paid part of the day's work now over, Julian seemed disinclined to do Linda any favors. Having no faith in his detective sense—or in any sense, for that matter—Simone decided she didn't need his help. She would take a quick look and then go see what Serge knew.

The LePage camp sat between the Thibodeau camp and the border, on lower land than Serge Thibodeau's—land that held water in wet springs with a resulting loss of vigor in the maple trees. Simone's grandfather and old LePage had started the camps together, leasing trees when sap was collected in buckets with horses and boiled over wood fires. The relative productivity of the neighboring stands had mattered less then, but with changing climate and changing markets, the marginal differences had amplified the gap in their respective commercial success. The transition that most camps had undergone, to vacuum-pulled plastic lines to collect the sap and all the trappings of a modern processing operation, had been easier for Simone's family than for the LePages. Now the LePage camp bore the marks of an unenthusiastic owner. While Serge, who had only ever wanted to run the family business, had modernized both home and equipment and expanded his lease to include good trees that stood on the ridge that ran right across the border, his contemporaries next door had done little to upgrade their camp.

The entrance to the LePage camp, visible from her uncle's short access road, had been plowed and driven on recently. Simone eased the truck's nose into the drive. She could hear a generator running and see a light on in the scruffy building that served as living quarters. No steam coming from the boiler vent so no boiling taking place, but this was not unreasonable. The Bolduc camps had not started boiling either, holding sap in big tanks for processing later, while the Morissettes had been in full boiling mode. Inching the truck a little farther into the LePage drive, Simone thought she saw the nose of a truck sticking out from behind the cabin. Okay, she thought, I can definitely tell Linda that there is some sort of action there. Let Robert work out the details next week. She felt no inclination to engage any LePage in conversation that would certainly be interpreted as snooping, and let the truck slide back onto the road. She pulled into the Thibodeau Érablière and poked Julian with her clip board.

"Ten minutes," she said. "There'll be coffee on. Come and be sociable for a quick visit. The border won't close for another half hour at least."

They pushed open the door to Serge's cabin, an expanded version of the original log camp that housed a comfortable collection of sofas around a wood stove, a bedroom almost entirely taken up by a queen size bed—a concession Serge had made to his wife, Marie-Noëlle, back when she had still been willing to spend weeks in the woods in maple season—and a bunkroom for helpers. A smell of wet dog rose from discarded wool socks and red plaid mackinaws draped over chair backs and a lop-sided clothes rack, its one broken leg propped on a family-sized can of baked beans.

Two bodies were draped across two sofas, their thumbs busy operating small screens. One of them, her cousin Mathieu, looked up as Simone walked in but avoided eye contact.

"Hi, handsome," she offered. "Serge around?" Mattie pointed to the sliding door that divided the living quarters from the working parts of the camp, his focus returning to his screen. She was used to his aversion to direct communication and his strange combination of uneven intelligence and social awkwardness. She sometimes wondered whether her whole damn family wasn't controlled by the same set of genes, which only expressed themselves so obviously in Mattie.

Leaving Julian to fill the remaining sofa, she joined Serge at the boiler, where a pan full of sap was now simmering gently and Serge was lining up new barrels to take the evening's product, shining a flashlight into each one to check for rust and chipping paint.

He looked up as Simone entered the building. Relations with his brother had soured many years ago, but he liked this tough girl and her preference for the woods life. She came up to help with tapping on short, freezing January days. Drilling holes in trees, inserting taps connected to the plastic lines that would carry the sap back to the camp was cold, hard work that few modern "kids" wanted to do. Having Simone there was a blessing. She could follow rules for tapping trees without supervision and thus without jeopardizing his organic status and costing him a valuable profit margin. Not to mention the loss of face he would suffer in this quality-driven business.

"Thought you weren't allowed near us," Serge commented as she stomped snow off her boots and pulled off her wool hat. The sugar house was a toasty, shirt-sleeve temperature as the big boiler was lit and the first pans of sap were almost done.

"Social call. We're just about outta here," she replied, "and I'm on a small busy-body mission. Linda called me, asked me to confirm that LePages are making syrup. You see anything happening there?" she asked.

"Try not to," was Serge's unhelpful reply. His shifty neighbors had been a source of irritation to him for years, threatening the pleasure he derived from his peaceful enterprise.

"Mattie goes over there when there's no-one around, looking for rats he can shoot. Place is a mess. But they were up tapping trees, so I guess they are making syrup."

He turned back to his task. "Mattie's in the camp. Go get him to make some coffee. I'm going to be up all night cooking this stuff. Sure you can't stay and help? Those boys are no damn good after they've eaten."

"Nah. We've got a day on the Baker Road tomorrow and reports to write. You oughta get Gilles up here—he's got nothing better to do." Her father had grown up in this business and could still be useful, she reckoned.

"Yeah, right," was all Serge had for comment. "Go bug Mattie. He'll be glad to see you. Make a change from not talking to me or his buddy there."

Mattie swung his legs off the sofa as Simone walked into the cabin.

"Hey," she greeted him. "Your grandfather told me to come and get coffee." Small talk was not Mattie's strength. Without responding, he got up and started opening cupboard doors, assembling filters and coffee for a thick, black, gut-scouring brew that, once sweetened with lashings of new syrup, would be their sustenance for the night's work. A big pie on the counter attested to her aunt's visit earlier in the day.

"Seen anything going on next door?" she asked. "I'm supposed to find out if they are using the camp."

"Using for what?" Mattie wanted to know.

Simone decided that whatever Mattie may be alluding to was way beyond her brief from Linda.

"Making syrup is all we care about," she replied. "MOMP wants to know if they should send an inspector in next week."

Mattie spoke directly to the coffee pot. "Want me to keep a lookout?" he asked. "I go over there some days to shoot rats. Haven't been since we started boiling on March 4." Just like him to have the date—probably the hour and minute, if she were to ask—that they started making syrup.

"Well, anything you can find out would be good. I was just there. Looks like someone is in there now but not much going on."

The second body shifted itself on the sofa and stood up, turning into the lanky form of Jean-Yves, Mattie's buddy from their middle-school Lego Club days.

"I can see what's up in their woods," he volunteered. "We check the back pump house every day anyway."

Jean-Yves's early fascination with models and electronic devices had morphed into a love affair with fast snow sleds and a facility for running pumps and generators. Simone guessed that his presence at the camp was due mostly to the appeal of the remoteness of the woods here, where he could run his noisy, souped-up machine without neighbors or parents bothering him. Serge had added a remote pump station when he had expanded his lease, and the daily task of checking that all was running smoothly was one more excuse for Jean-Yves to ride his jazzy toy into the woods.

"Had to fix the top dump tank this year." Mattie launched into a detailed description of the malfunctioning pump parts and their successful repairs. His mind stored detail in encyclopedic quantity, and he could regurgitate it without any processing or filter. Simone walked over and put an arm across his shoulders. She felt a wave of affection for her odd cousin. He flinched at her touch but she squeezed one arm gently and turned him around to face her.

"You are a babe," she said with a smile. "Let me know if you see anything funny, but don't go getting into trouble. You're going to be busy here."

"Okay. I'll text you if I have anything to report. I'd better tell Pépère the coffee is ready."

He had reached his limit for social interaction for now. The two of them joined Serge at the boiler. Sap was running well now and they would have a busy evening, concentrating and then boiling the sap that was filling huge storage tanks in the camp attic.

"I'm leaving," Simone announced, pulling her hat out of a pocket. "You guys have work to do." She hugged her uncle, who took his eye off his gadgets long enough to return the hug, and kiss her warmly on both cheeks.

"Tell your papa I could use his help. These boys poop out early and I'm getting old."

"I'll see what I can do. I'll see him tomorrow. Don't kill yourself. Sorry I can't stay and help, but the border's about to close so we gotta get going."

"*Sois sage, chérie,*" he told her.

"Always. Thanks. Be good yourself," she replied and headed back to the truck. She leaned on the horn and waited till the lumpen form of her copilot emerged from the cabin. Still plenty of time to cross back into Canada, despite the deteriorating roads. The warming temperatures had brought snow, falling steadily now and, if the weather forecast was to be trusted, due to continue all night. That would make tomorrow a slog, as the rural roads in Canada got little attention from snow plows late in the winter and the Baker Road would, most likely, be a troublesome mix of new snow over muddy ruts. Simone decided against feeling sorry for herself, choosing instead a comfortably smug recognition that she could handle shitty roads under almost any conditions and hoping that Julian would be suitably impressed.

2

The warm-stove crowd of retirees who met around the corner table of the Moose Crossing Café in Jackman was in a somber mood. This is hunting-camp country, alive with camo-clad sports from Bangor and beyond in deer and moose season and maintaining a steady pulse through bird-hunting, fishing, and snowmobiling months. But in mud season, when the ice is treacherous and snow acquires the consistency of mashed potatoes, only the hardy—or those too dull to leave—remain.

The conversation, which had centered around strategies to avoid getting busted by state troopers when hauling overweight loads of logs, turned to plans for fishing as soon as the ice went out of the ponds and lakes, still weeks away but always on their minds.

Gilles Thibodeau (Gill to his Anglophone colleagues and friends who could not handle the soft French "G") stared at the morning's *New York Times* crossword—downloaded and printed out before he left his camp, now abandoned out of boredom and frustration on the table beside him.

"Shit, boys, I'm beginning to wonder if retirement was such a good idea," he said, dumping another packet of sugar into his cup of black coffee. After a couple of hours on the warmer, the stuff had acquired interesting top notes of acid and shoe polish. "My energy levels are all to hell and I've started to hate this damned snow. Used to like it. Now it gets me down."

"Oh, quit your whining. You're a lucky man. I thought you and Jocelyne were making the best of cold nights, anyway," replied the small man beside him. Richard Martin, retired high school math teacher, had recently celebrated forty-five years of marriage to his college girlfriend, whose plump form could be found sorting clothes and handing out donated food at the Jackman Thrift shop Saturday mornings, Monday afternoons, and every other Wednesday. Nobody doubted that they still kept each other warm.

"Shit," Gilles repeated. "If making the best of cold nights means two Advil PMs and a lot of bad dreams, I guess you could say so. Don't know why the woman stays with me. I quit being any fun months ago. She should find herself someone her own age."

"What do you mean, her own age? She was in Madeleine's class, and that's only six years after us."

"Yeah, well, I guess six years makes a difference when it comes to—oh, what the hell, I'm old and tired and no use to a woman anymore."

"You should go down to Florida with Annie and Ray," his friend suggested. Raymond and Annie Pray had run a sporting camp in the area for thirty years, but now spent the winters in Florida and much of the summer touring National Parks in their outsize motor home.

"Yeah, and feel like a damn fool surrounded by geezers like us, all getting wrinkly in the sun. I'd rather be in the woods. And what's Florida going to do for me? It's going to take a whole lot more than a bunch of babes on the beach to get me back into the game."

Failing to extract any further response from the group, he crumpled the crossword into a ball and fed it to the wood stove. He added an old canvas jacket to his layers of clothes and turned to leave.

"Simone's due in tomorrow. I should go pull some moose steaks out of the freezer."

That got renewed attention from the stove-huggers.

"What time's dinner?" and "Mine's medium rare—plenty of onions," came his way as he opened the door to the icy mess that passed for a sidewalk. Snow was falling in fat, wet flakes, confirming the ugly truth that April is still a winter month in the north of Maine.

"In your dreams. I need some quality time with the kid. But I'll let you know when I turn the tough bits into a stew someday."

He coaxed reluctant life out of his aged Jeep and headed home. Two miles from the village center he turned onto a rough dirt road, at the entrance to which a plywood sign announced "You are now 75 miles from the nearest stop light." Half a mile in from the highway he pulled up to the front of his camp, a log structure that he had built over thirty years earlier during his first sabbatical from the University of Maine.

Now that he had settled into his second year of retirement, he found this simple life and admittedly primitive dwelling entirely to his liking. Since giving up, with no hint of regret, on his professional life, he had spent a year upgrading the old hunting camp into his idea of a perfect retirement home. He had not initially intended to abandon the small apartment in Bangor that had housed him since his divorce, but after a year of driving up to Jackman to work on the camp he had realized that it was all he needed, and the sense of complete removal from all obligations to former students, projects, and even friends suited him well. He felt at home in the woods, and found he preferred the company of the folks up here than that of the academics with whom he had spent forty working years. He had grown up like this, and it felt like home.

Recently, he had begun to wonder about repairing the somewhat fractured relationship with his brother. He realized that they intimidated each other, he by his education and assimilation into the world of American university life, Serge by his loyalty to his backwoods French origins. They were both accustomed to accusing each other of not working as hard as they felt they each did, and the tension had built over the years into an abrasive mutual distrust. But days spent fixing the cabin, working up the cords of firewood he would use each winter, filling his freezer with whatever he could kill during the assorted hunting seasons that he was now free to enjoy had softened his view of his brother's choices. Even without the complicated business of running a modern sugaring operation, the self-sufficient life in the woods was not an easy one. The skills that he had employed all his life, building and dismantling stage sets for the Theatre Department, had all been initially learned as a boy helping with the family business, but he knew that he would be out of his depth if asked to run the sophisticated equipment that Serge now used. His recent upgrade to the cabin—installing a generator and wiring so he could run a freezer and power tools—had been a challenge, and as he contemplated a project that would give him running hot and cold water, he wondered whether asking Serge for help would be a way to restore a bond that had existed many years ago. Life here was good, and it might be made better by getting to know his brother and family again.

And then there was Jocelyne. He had not been looking for romance, or even for sex, since peace and freedom from expectations had been his priorities for what he saw as the next and possibly best phase of his life. But what had started as a few conversations had unexpectedly turned into a surprisingly satisfying friendship, with a lot of unmistakably splendid benefits. He wondered what she was up to, but had to cut that line of thinking off short. Simone had called from Saint-Georges. She and the dope from MOMP who was inspecting with her would be here tomorrow, and he had plans for a pot of beans and a pan of cornbread to go with his prized moose steaks. He recognized that he didn't have a lot to say to his edgy daughter, and that she was mostly mad at him for her unstable childhood, but they had found common ground when out in the woods together, and he knew she would enjoy the steaks. He decided he would make a serious effort to talk to her. It was not lost on him that she was closer to her uncle than he was, and that she would rather spend time up at the sugar camp than with her father. He would find out from her how things were going on the Golden Road, and maybe follow up on the idea of making overtures to Serge.

Once the moose steaks had been selected, beans set out to soak, and the dust swept off the floor of his "guest" loft, Gilles pulled out his laptop and clicked through the latest Netflix offerings. He paused at a potentially promising Derek Jacobi series. Checking the brief synopsis, he was annoyed to find that it was yet another piece pandering to the oldies, whom, he supposed, made up the bulk of the Netflix watchers. Wikipedia filled him in on the details: it was a last-ditch romance story of two old friends who meet up and find love and cuddling followed by family problems and heart failure. What a waste of a fine actor, one whom Gilles had followed for most of their more-or-less concurrent careers. Do we really need proof that we are still sexy? he asked the laptop screen. Only the other day, some article he had read had breathlessly reported that the Boomer generation was getting it on like no group their age had ever done before. No shit, he thought, and I don't need the *Huffington Post* or Derek Jacobi to tell me. Jocelyne's presence had spiced up his life, but he was in no mood to be reminded of the problem that haunted him now as he thought of her. The popular cliché, that sex, like riding a bicycle, was something you never forgot how to do, was all well and good as long as you had any air in the tires.

Giving up on the hope of a decent movie, and recognizing that a day cleaning up the winter's firewood remains and pulling canoes and paddles out of the shed in preparation for ice-out and some good fishing, had left him smelling like a goat, Gilles shed his clothes in a pile and padded into what passed for his bathroom—a curtained-off corner of the cabin. The appliances were currently limited to a large enamel bowl on a couple of milk crates, filled via bucket from water heated on the wood stove. He caught sight of his naked self in the long mirror on the wall and stopped to reflect on the fact that with oncoming old age his body was becoming that of an orangutan. He had never thought of himself as bowlegged, but there was definitely something ape-like about his stance now. Add to this a somewhat protruding paunch, barrel chest, a disappearing ass, and a sag of skin under his chin that occupied the place where his neck had been, and the resemblance to a tree-dwelling cousin was remarkable. He rounded his shoulders and swung his arms experimentally. Yup, the *vieux singe* look was his to wear. Too bad, he told himself, straightening up, sucking in the gut and squaring his shoulders back to where they ought to be. It all still works—or most of it.

As he toweled himself dry and dusted the moving parts with powder, he wondered whether Jocelyne had told him what she was up to tonight. He decided against finding out, and having topped up the beans for a good overnight soak, he burrowed into the pile of blankets on his bed and hoped for a dreamless sleep. He resolved to focus his limited abilities as a communicator on his family, and hope that whatever good came of that might transfer to his relationship with Jocelyne.

* * *

The setting sun put a nasty glare on the icy road into Jackman. The day of inspections on the Baker Road had been hard work, as anticipated. Heavy, wet snow from the day before had made driving tricky, and Simone was tired—tired of being unfairly in charge of the job, tired of bad roads, poor food, and the effort of speaking French. But the inspection needs had been met, camps all seen as scheduled and only the day's reports to complete. They could wait.

With the big Armstrong border station behind them and her father's cabin a short distance ahead, she was ready to be rid of Julian and work. He had been in conversational mode on the road back from Saint-Georges. It had started with his tiresome and unnecessarily detailed answer to the border guard's questions. She had merely handed over her passport and the information that they had been doing maple syrup inspections for MOMP in the camps along the Baker and Golden roads. Julian's fulsome explanations of their need to stay in Saint-Georges in order to access the camps on the Maine side of the border were redundant. These guys know all that shit already, she told herself. He's just showing off. No surprise. It got worse as they drove into Jackman. His pompous assertions of superior knowledge about the maple business and his need to criticize every camp and operator they had visited caused a significant rise in her blood pressure. You try working as hard as those guys, she wanted to say. They bust ass from January to mid-May every year, stuck out in the woods, needing the skills of engineers, foresters, food-processors, businessmen, and back-country survivors through four months of hard weather and isolation. It takes a lot more than one frat boy's knowledge to make a living at this game, and she wished he would shut up and recognize the improbability of ever working that hard. The upcoming night in Jackman was beginning to feel like a break. Dealing with her father would not necessarily be easy, but at least it would be a change.

Once her phone indicated reasonable reception, Simone checked calls and messages. There was a text from Jocelyne, her father's newish girlfriend, that simply said "Call me when you can." Punching the Call button, she heard the phone ring and Jocelyne's voice, sounding relieved, answered.

"Simone, hi, how's them woods?" the now-familiar voice asked.

"Muddy, cold, beautiful," Simone answered. "What's up?"

Jos called occasionally to chat. She and Simone's father had been "seeing" each other (Simone tried not to picture it) for a couple of years, and she and Simone had established a loose but friendly relationship.

"Have you talked to your dad recently?" Jos asked.

"Not really. Why?"

"Oh, nothing I can put my finger on. I just wondered if you had any idea what's going on with him."

"Not a clue. You know he never tells me anything." Simone's desire to get involved with her father's state of mind was somewhere below minimal, but she liked Jocelyne, who seemed to have a better approach than most to dealing with the man she had taken up with, and after two years, Simone was beginning to believe that this one might stick.

"Oh that's just not true. You are one of the few people he does talk to."

Simone's fellow-feeling for any woman trying to make sense out of a relationship with a man—something she felt she had failed at in numerous and spectacular ways—overrode her distaste for any involvement with her father's love life. She ignored the sharp thump under her ribs, her ever-ready anxiety response to any reminder of her tension-filled efforts to communicate with her father.

"So what's he been up to?" she dared to ask. She held her breath, waiting to hear once again that her father was betraying a nice woman, his promises, and, above all, his daughter.

"Oh, I don't know, but he seems to be sad lately. Or sick. Or something. Won't admit to anything and I don't want to nag." Sickness would be an improvement, Simone thought. Something she could deal with.

"Jeez. He hasn't said a word to me. I've been stuck up in maple camps all week but I'm just headed there now. You not going to be there?"

"No." There was a pause. "No," Jocelyne repeated, "but let me know if you pick up on anything serious."

"Well, sure, but don't hold your breath. Heart-to-heart with Father is not my best thing."

"Yeah, I know—but still. Hope you don't mind my mentioning it. It's probably nothing. Either way, take care."

The call ended, leaving Simone with an awkward sense of a boundary crossed. She focused on the lousy driving conditions, a problem that felt a lot more familiar and solvable. At this time of year, the road from the border into Jackman became a horrifying series of frost heaves—irregularly spaced humps and mini-ravines that, taken at speed in a stiff-suspensioned truck, could bounce you up to the cab roof. Julian roused himself to cinch his seat belt and Simone contemplated hitting a few bumps hard enough to shake him.

They drove past the entrances to the multitude of sporting camps that lay between the border and the town of Jackman, turning at last into the camp road. At the entrance to the camp, a broken sign made of birch twigs nailed to a rough board read Thibodeau G.

The only indication that Gilles was around was the noisy thrumming of the generator. Not stopping to look for him, Simone started unloading her co-pilot's possessions and throwing them into the back of his vehicle, a hybrid sedan that was clearly a hand-me-down from his mother. About as much use as its owner, in Simone's opinion. She suppressed the twinge of guilt she felt about not offering food or a beer before he hit the road, but she had had enough of his company for a good while and much preferred the thought of a beer consumed without him. As he backed the car out onto the camp road, she was forced to admit that the seventy-five miles or so of lousy road that separated Jackman from Skowhegan would be a bitch under the current conditions. Snow was beginning to fall again. It would be turning to rain and slush as he traveled south, but, hey, he was no longer her problem, and his choice of vehicle was his to deal with. She picked up the backpack that she hoped still had a change of underwear and her toothbrush in it, and went to face her next interpersonal challenge.

Her father emerged from the camp with the news that beans and a steak awaited her, and half an hour and two beers later she had unwound enough to attempt a conversation. She found her father's company awkward. While she had learned from him how to love, and live in, the wilderness, she did not trust him on any personal or emotional matters. She had suffered through an unstable childhood, all of which she blamed on his drinking, his serial girlfriends, constant absences from home, and her mother's resultant fury and despair. They had finally, mercifully, divorced when Simone was in middle school, after a sabbatical trip he had made to England, returning with a newly recruited female grad student. Although tensions had eased, Simone's sense of abandonment and disappointment had barely shifted in the now more than twelve years since the divorce. He's a self-absorbed ass, was her usual assessment of him, but the hope that one day they would actually share a better relationship tugged at her.

"Serge says he could really use your help," was her opening move, after they had exhausted road conditions and weather as conversation topics. "Sap is running and he's only got Mattie and Jean-Yves up there. Not much of a crew if he gets busy. Think you still know how to make syrup?"

Gilles's reply was surprisingly humble. "Well, I guess I can follow instructions. Can't have changed that much."

Odd, Gilles thought, that he had just been thinking about his brother. Maybe this was the chance he had been looking for. A few days working together might be just what they both needed. At least it would get him out of the sorry mood he had been in lately. It was common knowledge that the big syrup camps were suffering from crippling labor shortages, the measly visa quota for Canadian workers having been used up long before the needs of the syrup industry had been met. The majority of the camp operators were Canadian citizens, dependent on family and friends from Canada to meet their brief seasonal need for workers, but even family members had been unable to get work permits this year. Caught between xenophobic government restrictions on "foreign" workers and a non-existent supply of capable or even available workers from the sparsely populated American side of the border, the camps were hurting and Gilles's advantage to his brother, as an American citizen, was not lost on either of them.

"Got no way to get up there, is the thing," he said. "Damn Jeep is on its last wheels."

Simone followed his glance through the window to where his ancient and unsightly Army Jeep sat.

"Transmission is almost gone, and the starter is just about shot. I'll fix it when the weather gets better, but for now—" He was about to confess that he was relying on Jocelyne for transportation beyond the bar and the hardware store, but a quick look at his daughter's disapproving face told him that admitting to his inadequate vehicle was going to be enough for one evening.

"Can't one of your buddies take you in?" Simone suggested. "There's no way Serge can come get you."

"Nah. Shit—would take a lot more than a needy sugar camp to shift those guys from the stove. And Jocelyne is working, and besides, her car is not made for those roads."

A long pause followed while they both wondered how best to address the obvious solution to this dilemma. Simone was damned if she was going to offer taxi service, but had no good response to her father's next question.

"What's up for you next few days?" he asked, hoping it sounded like an unrelated topic.

"Just checking in at MOMP. I need to get today's reports done. Maybe go see Mom," was the best that Simone could come up with.

"So run me in to Serge's and I'll buy you a tank of gas."

Unable to think of a defensible reason for not agreeing, and with the memory of her uncle's plea for help calling on her better nature, she settled on establishing conditions.

"Okay. But we have to get going early so I can go home down the Golden Road. It won't be too bad in the morning." Taking the logging road back to Millinocket was technically a short cut, but late winter conditions could make the almost hundred-mile trek a challenge at best. The recent cold weather meant that the road had been kept plowed and passable, and even with the new snow, driving wouldn't be too bad. Despite being a privately owned road, it was a major throughway and way better maintained than the side roads to the camps. With an early start, she should be able to make it down to Bangor in under four hours. The prospect of the long, solitary drive through the woods appealed to her. There would be no logging traffic, and the last time she had driven this road in late winter she had encountered flocks of crossbills scavenging for grit on the gravel road. You never knew what interesting nonhuman life forms you might find on the long trip through the woods. At this time of year, moose were beginning to move around and might be spotted along the road. Plus, if she had to drive Gilles up to the sugar camp, she could postpone her promised investigation of his state of mind until the morning. Added to that, she liked the idea that he would be facing some hard work if the sap flow kept up. Given her weariness and her reluctance to spoil the relatively serene evening, the deal seemed like a good one, so with a promise of an early start, she climbed up to the loft and was soon asleep.

* * *

It was still dark when she awoke. The sleeping bag was a cocoon-like haven, but the smell of bacon, coffee, and Gilles's waffles, stacked on an old baking sheet on the wood stove, got her out of the loft and off to the outhouse. Gilles's plans for upgraded plumbing in the camp did not run to a real flush. He liked the outhouse and didn't much care for people who didn't.

"How's the temperature?" he asked as she came back in, knocking snow off her boots. "Thought you might find it kinda cold—on the whole."

She suppressed any reaction, unwilling to acknowledge his stupid double-entendre jokes. Breakfast was another matter, and she surprised herself by volunteering that it was better than Mme Rodrigue's offerings at the *gîte* in Saint-Georges. Starting the day without a fight was progress, and she held on to the mellow mood as they filled the back of her truck with Gilles's clutter. Her anticipation of a slow day's drive by herself, once she had dropped him off at Serge's, was all the motivation she needed to overlook her father's disorganized approach to the trip. While he threw random assortments of tools, clothes, and food into the truck, she mapped out her day in her mind. She had relayed her observations of some inspection-worthy activity at the LePage camp to Linda and had reported that she was headed back to the Golden Road as her father's Uber. She would stop for a snack and a quick visit at Serge's—catch up on anything the boys had to report after two warm, sap-producing days had passed—and then look forward to hours of peace as she made her way back across Maine. It would ease her return to civilization, report-writing, and the question of what to do with her oncoming summer and the money she had earned from the maple season work.

Once on the road, headed for the Armstrong border crossing, Gilles pulled out his phone and punched up a call. Simone found herself the unwilling eavesdropper on her father's apologetic call to Jocelyne. Evidently they had not talked for a while, and they had not discussed his hurried plan to go help his brother.

"She's mad at me." He pulled a face as he pushed his phone back into a breast pocket.

"I know. Talked to her last night. What the hell have you done to piss her off?" She felt she had promised Jos to make at least minimal inquiries, and a small part of her guiltily relished her father's obvious discomfort.

"Oh, I don't know. Not her fault. My problem, I guess. Not much of a boyfriend." Gilles's mumbled explanations made no sense to Simone.

"What the hell are you talking about? You must have done something dumb. Even you should be able to figure that out." Her impatience with an inarticulate man overrode her distaste for the conversation. Why did it always have to fall to women to work out what the hell was going on in the world of relationships? Not that she had any great skills in this realm.

"More likely what I can't do," Gilles offered to the passenger side window.

"What do you mean, what can't you do?" The conversation was headed in a confessional direction that made her uncomfortable, but she was in it now.

"Getting old. Not much good to a woman anymore," was all she got back.

"What in the world does that mean?" Simone wanted to know. "Can't be a big surprise to Jos that you are an old fart. She's going on sixty herself. What's that got to do with anything? You talk to her about this at all?"

"Not really. I guess I'm not much good at this stuff." Gilles continued to address the passenger side window.

"No shit," Simone agreed, as they sunk into a welcome silence.

Once through the border, and with an hour of driving still ahead of them, she dug into the pouch of CDs her father had tossed onto the dashboard as they left. Radio up here was for shit—a few Bible-thumping stations, the worst country biker-music, and bits of jumpy French talk radio. She flipped through some nerdy jazz and a bunch of '60s rock, paused to consider *Dark Side of the Moon*, and passed on, fearing it would start Gilles on tedious recollections of his sex-drugs-and-rock-and-roll student days. She settled on some anodyne piano sonatas and turned her attention to the slippery roads.

As they approached Saint-Georges, a stunningly ugly banana-yellow Humvee roared past them on a blind curve, cutting in front of the truck and spraying a sticky mess of snow and salty road grit onto the windshield. Gilles came half out of his seat, gesticulating furiously at the departing Hummer, both middle fingers waving at the offensive road hog.

"Those motherfucking cocksuckers," he exploded. "Fuck them and the goddamn blow job they rode in on."

"Know them?" Simone asked, as she silently gave her father credit for knowing his way around urban dictionary vulgarisms.

"Know them? They fucking robbed me. Bastard LePage assholes. Never worth the space they took up. Hope they die an ugly death. And soon."

"Jeez. What did they do to you?"

Gilles had sunk back into his seat and seemed reluctant to expand any further on the LePages' transgressions, but Simone's interest was now piqued. This was the second time in as many days that the LePages had come up as sources of trouble.

"No, seriously, what have they done to get you so mad at them?" she asked.

"Bastards can't keep a promise," was all she got, so she pressed further.

"What promise?"

"Ah, shit. They were running blue pills in for us, if you must know, but they wrapped up their business and left us hanging."

"Pills? Business? What the hell?" Simone had no idea what he was talking about, for the second time that morning.

Something about his impatient daughter's judgmental attitude prompted a desire to shock her—an impulse he regretted as soon as he heard the words leave his mouth.

"Cheap Canadian Viagra, okay? They were bringing us bootleg pills so we didn't have to ask Ed for them."

Oh, sweet Jesus, she thought, don't tell me I am getting an erectile dysfunction confession from my parent.

"So what happened?" she asked, hoping to keep the focus on the LePages.

"I guess they've moved on to harder drugs. But they kept a bunch of our money."

This was followed by an awkward silence while Simone fought with the idea that 'hard' drugs were exactly what he had been buying. Then a thought struck her.

"That why you are running away from Jos?" she asked. She got no answer, but his embarrassed face told her she had hit a mark. What jerks men are, she thought, utterly disgusted by him and regretting her decision to drive him up to the camp.

"Seriously?" she asked. "You think that matters? What kind of an ass are you? Jos likes you, for chrissakes. You think she gives a shit about—?" She could not bring herself to get into any detail. "Jesus, *Father*," she added, hoping that the emphasis would remind him of their basic relationship and the inappropriateness of this conversation. "Why would you fuck up a good thing over something that dumb?"

They lapsed back into familiar tense silence, the piano sonatas now more of an irritant than a distraction. She hit the eject button and focused on her driving, turning onto the Saint-Zacharie road just before reaching Saint-Georges. The further they got from the main road, the more prevalent became the patches of ice and snow left behind by the snow plows. The surprisingly heavy traffic on the little road added to the challenge, but at least her father had the class not to offer advice on her driving. Silence reigned until they reached the border crossing at Saint-Zacharie.

Haskell was at his usual post. In the presence of her father, Simone found herself reluctant to talk to him, and handed over her passport without making eye contact as she made her customary beeline for the bathroom. To her disgust, Gilles and Haskell were chatting like old friends when she came out. Hey, she thought, get away from him. None of your damned business making friends here. Wanting to escape the recognition that this was an entirely irrational reaction, she hurried her father into the truck and onto the road.

"Nice guy. Steve. Lives in Albion," Gilles reported. It annoyed Simone that her father had found out these details in two minutes, end-running her poorly formed but elaborate plans to glean them for herself. She comforted herself with the thought of the day ahead. Quick stop, grab a coffee, and I will be free of men, work, and family for a whole day, she thought.

* * *

When they pulled in to Serge's camp, there was no steam rising from the sugar house, so they ventured into the cabin to find all three guys asleep— fully clad, blankets piled over them, and the fire in the wood stove a mere memory. Evidence of a hasty meal consumed sometime during the night's work was piled on the table. One look at Gilles's face told Simone that housekeeping was not what he had signed up for. She shoved a handful of kindling at him and motioned toward the near-dead stove, as she gathered up dishes and started throwing pizza crusts and empty chip packets into the garbage. Figuring she should have a word with Mattie before she left, and that making coffee would be the best way to get the sleepers back on their feet, she activated the coffee maker and poked around in the fridge for something that might be healthier than the meal these guys had thought would sustain them the night before. Before long, the three bodies had become sleepy consumers of coffee and toast. Serge's relief and pleasure at his brother's arrival was proof of the pressure he was under.

"Can't believe you made it so soon, *vieille branche,*" he said, interrupting a gesture that might have become a brotherly hug. Not ready for that. He put an arm around Simone instead.

"Thank you, *chérie,* for bringing him up here. It's a mess out there. We filled seven barrels last night and left all the cleanup for this morning. Burned the big pan a bit last night—not too bad, but it's going to need some work, and we're going to get busy again."

After another night of snow, the temperature was already working its way into the forties and sap would run fast if that trend continued. Serge ran his fingers through his mess of tangled hair and sighed. Getting all the equipment cleaned and into shape for another big boil would take several hours, and Simone knew she couldn't drive away until she had offered to help get them up and running. She followed her uncle and father out to the boiler room, still warm from the night's work. The caramel smell of burnt sugar and an array of sticky equipment greeted them, confirming her realization that she would have to stay awhile longer.

Clean hot water is always in plentiful supply after a syrup run, generated from the reverse-osmosis process and the condensation of the steam from boiling down the concentrated sap. Leaving the two brothers to wrestle with the big pan and set it up under the automated washer, Simone turned to dismantling the press filter and removing the blocks of sticky diatomaceous earth now trapped behind the row of paper filters. Mattie stumbled into the sugar house looking for her, and the high-pitched scream of a souped-up snowmobile engine told her that Jean-Yves was getting ready to run up to the far pump house to check on heaters and pumps.

"Not going up with him?" Simone asked her cousin. His preference was for snow shoes and quiet, but a fast run up the road to the pump house was always fun, and a way to get out of camp cleaning chores.

"Too noisy," was Mattie's reply. "And he can go faster by himself." He picked up a dropped wing nut from the press and coughed.

"LePages are making syrup," he offered. "They've been busy up at the top."

"Oh. Cool. Thanks for the update. I'll tell Linda. Good work."

Simone was going to leave it at that, but Mattie was uncharacteristically forthcoming with more information.

"We went up to see what they've been doing after you were here. They've been working up there. I think they are repairing lines or something."

Mattie seemed keen to prove that he had taken his promise to check out the neighbors' activities seriously. The simple fact that they were indeed making syrup was enough information for Simone, so she steered Mattie's moment of communicative energy to questions about Jean-Yves's fancy snow machine.

"It's an Arctic Cat XF 1100 Turbo SnoPro," Mattie reported, never short of detail on any topic that he encountered. "He can get it over a hundred on a good road."

"Wow, that fast." She did a quick conversion in her mind: At 100 kph, the boy was topping seventy miles an hour. Scary. "He let you drive it?" she asked.

"Don't want to. I take Pépère's Polaris," he answered.

"Smart guy." The utility sled, reliable but unexciting, was used for all the woods work. Simone approved of Mattie's cautious approach to life. Here was one guy who didn't need to show off on a giant machine to prove his value to the world.

Simone took a long look around the sugar house. Order was on the way to being restored. Serge had the wash-and-rinse process running on the R/O membranes. The big pan was fine and could be reinstalled in the boiler as soon as all the crust was washed out. The seven barrels from last night were labeled and logged into the records, and Serge and Gilles seemed to be working together surprisingly well. No way the inspector next week was going to find anything wrong there. Every barrel had to be accounted for and traceable back to the day it was made. Robert would be here soon and checking production logs.

She could hear sap beginning to run into the holding tanks in the attic of the camp, a trickle that would soon be gushing. The heavy overcast day had developed into light snow, reducing visibility and threatening slippery roads with the slowly rising temperature. Time to hit the road.

"I'm headed," she called across to them. "You guys gonna manage without me?"

"We'll try. How about you make us another pot of coffee before you go?" her father called back.

She swallowed a tart "You can't make your own coffee?" retort. They were busy, loading new filter papers into the press, and Mattie was fiddling with dials in the R/O room—and besides, a new cup of hot coffee would be welcome on the road. In the cabin, she fed logs into the stove, cleaned up the breakfast remains, kicked a pile of malodorous clothes into the bunkroom, and waited for the coffee to brew. With a travel mug full of hot caffeine and a candy bar from the cabin's deep resources, she went back in search of the guys.

"Call Jocelyne, and don't be an ass about it," she told Gilles. She gave her uncle a quick hug, sought out Mattie for a goodbye tap on his arm, and was rearranging the mess in her truck when Gilles came shuffling across the ice to find her, zipping up a heavy jacket and pulling gloves and a hat out of the pockets.

"Hey," he said. "You got a few minutes? Serge is wondering what's happened to Jean-Yves. It shouldn't take him this long to check the pump house. He's been gone over half an hour. Serge wants someone to go check on him. You know the place better than I do. I've never been up to the new pump station, and…" He trailed off, leaving the request for backup on the mission hanging.

"Mattie?" Simone asked.

"He's busy in the R/O room. Serge doesn't want to worry him. But it's weird that Jean-Yves isn't back yet. Run up and check it out with me. You've still got plenty of time."

Whatever, she thought. A small part of her was pleased that Gilles wanted her company. Donning her own layer of outerwear, she followed Gilles to where the big Polaris sat ready.

"You drive," she said. "Straight up behind the camp. I'll shout when we need to turn."

The remote pump house was positioned on a flat spot just below the ridge that ran across to the border. Serge had added it when he had expanded his lease to include the high trees. The access road climbed a low rise and then forked left to run the quarter mile to the pump house, encircling the easternmost stand of the LePages' trees. At the sedate pace that Gilles drove the heavy snowmobile, Simone could see the LePages' sap lines. She noted sagging, dirty tubing and wondered whether this would draw comment from Robert when he inspected the business next week. Old tubing wasn't a disqualifier for organic certification, but it indicated poor management. Bacteria develop in sap that sits in sagging lines, and old connections cause air leaks that reduce the vacuum pressure. The results are lower yields and poorer quality syrup. Not her problem, she reminded herself, though she would pass on the observation to Linda when she got back to MOMP. Meanwhile, the sled was rounding the bend that would lead to the last straightaway to the pump house.

She felt the shock in her father's body before she had a chance to look over his shoulder to see what had caused it. As Gilles swung the sled off the road and killed the engine, she heard a voice that sounded a lot like her own cry out, "Holy fucking shit!" Ahead of them, fifty yards or so up the straight track, the jazzy stripes of Jean-Yves's Arctic Cat were visible partway up a leaning tree, its mangled skis caught in the branches. A few yards closer to them, a twisted body lay motionless in the snow, its head at an awkward angle. Across the path a stout cable swung a couple of feet into the air.

Simone found herself unable to move, unable to understand what she was seeing. Gilles was struggling to get off the snowmobile, encumbered by Simone's body on the seat behind him. She could hear him shouting, "Shit, shit, shit," but it took several more seconds before she could make her limbs move.

3

Before Simone could conquer her paralysis, Gilles had reached the body and was carefully unzipping the neck of the snowsuit to feel for a pulse. He looked up at Simone, still standing by the snowmobile, and shook his head as he caught her eye.

"He's not breathing. Can't feel a pulse." He left the obvious conclusion unstated. "Go get help," he added. "I'll stay here."

Simone's mind was beginning to clear, and was forming a picture of herself walking into the camp with the news of what they had just found. She knew she couldn't do this alone, and her shaking limbs gave her no sense of being able to control the heavy sled.

"Shit, Dad, no. You have to come with me." She hadn't called her father "Dad" in over a decade, and hearing herself say this brought a sharp recognition of the horror of what they were facing.

"Nothing you can do here," she pointed out, as the ability to think returned slowly, "and Mattie—"

She didn't finish the sentence, but they both knew what she was thinking. Gilles zipped the snowsuit back up and walked the few yards back to the snowmobile. He motioned Simone out of the way as he turned the machine around, and, as she settled onto the passenger seat behind him, started slowly back the way they had come. Simone found herself wanting to wrap her arms around her father, and settled instead for folding them against his back and leaning her head on them as they made their way back to the camp. A plan was forming in her mind, fueled by the knowledge that they needed help from someone, anyone, who knew how to deal with the awfulness of this situation. Serge had no reliable means of communication at the camp. If he needed anything at all, he would drive to the border where cell phones worked and call Marie-Noëlle. Haskell, she thought to herself. He will know what to do.

On reaching the camp, Simone made a beeline for her truck.

"I'm going to get help," she shouted, leaving Gilles to do what she knew she couldn't, breaking the news to Serge and Mattie. It took a mere fifteen minutes to reach the border station, and as she stumbled into the building she was begging the universe that he would be there, alone, with an established protocol ready to go that would make this all seem handle-able.

He registered surprise as she half fell through the door. Maple syrup inspectors, especially this one, were not typically given to dramatic entrances. Before he could form a question, she had started to blurt out half-formed statements of disaster. He waited, and as the need to communicate clearly fought its way through to the front of her mind, she managed an explanation of her chaotic appearance.

"There's been an accident. It's Jean-Yves. He came off his snowmobile up by the pump house. I think he must have broken his neck or something, but he's..."

Haskell's response was blessedly calm.

"Tell me again," he said, "only slower, so I understand."

"He went up to check the pump house this morning and wasn't back when we expected him, so my father and I went to see what was going on and we found him on the road. Looks like he ran into a cable and it took him off the snow machine. He drives that stupid thing like a race car and in the snow you can't see a damned thing anyway." She wanted to be mad that the kid had put himself in harm's way with his idiotic need for speed.

Haskell wanted only the facts. He pulled out a chair beside his desk and guided Simone into it.

"So, do you need a doctor? I can call and see if anyone—" He wasn't ready for the sharp wail of her response that cut off his question.

"Jesus, no, he's dead, for chrissakes. My dad couldn't find a pulse. He was—" She could find no words to describe the doll-like appearance of the boy as he lay on the snow, his head on all wrong, and no semblance of the kid she had talked to barely over an hour earlier.

"Then I need to call the State Police. Everything goes through them." To Simone's huge relief, he was offering reassuring professionalism rather than useless sympathy. She heard his voice over the pounding of her heart.

"This is Border Control Agent Steven Haskell at the Saint-Zacharie border station. I am reporting a snowmobile accident and what appears to be an unattended death on the Golden Road in T5 R20."

Hearing him identify the place by its Township and Range lines, the only name many of the lined-out, unincorporated spaces in the top half of Maine have, brought home to Simone the remoteness of the place. How the hell are we going to deal with this, with no fucking cell phone service and no way for help to reach us? her racing mind asked. Through the clouds of despair that were settling over her, she heard the measured voice of Steve Haskell.

"They need to know exactly where the accident occurred," he was saying. She managed to produce Serge's camp number, and listened again as Steve relayed the information to the dispatcher.

He hung up the phone and reported the other half of the conversation.

"They are sending the game warden, and say someone needs to be there to take him to the accident site."

"Serge and my father are there, but I need to get back too." She stood up and was grateful to her knees for supporting her. As she made for the door, Haskell came around the counter that acted as his desk and put a hand out to her shoulder. Aware that he had done nothing but provide prompt and useful help, she looked up and found a concerned and friendly face looking for ways to offer more personal aid.

"You okay?" he asked, pulling the door open. She hoped that gratitude for his reasonable presence showed on her face, which felt entirely frozen.

"Yup. I'm—thanks." Words weren't working well, and the best she could manage was repetition. "Thank you. I'll—" "I'll be in touch" sounded too stupid to utter, like something you might say after someone had dropped off a dish of food, so she said nothing but let him close the truck door as she started the engine.

The short drive back to the camp gave her time to face the one thought she had been avoiding: Mattie. There was no way he was going to be able to handle this. He needed predictability and routine, and even slight mishaps could derail him. Since middle school, Jean-Yves had been his only real friend. They shared an obsession with mechanical details and a certain sense of removal from the regular world. They had graduated from high school together almost a year earlier and had mostly worked for Serge in the interval. The shock of his buddy's death (was that really what had just happened, Simone asked herself?) would be a catastrophe for Mattie's fragile hold on his place in life.

Gilles was standing by the camp door when she stopped the truck in the yard. His face had the stricken, dead look that she felt had taken over her whole body, but he stepped toward her and nodded at the camp as she asked, "Mattie?"

"Serge's with him. I was waiting for you. What's…?"

"Game warden on his way," Simone interrupted. "They said to wait where he can find us easily."

The rest of that day passed in a dense fog of misery, with peaks of sharper awfulness breaking through the clouds. The game warden, reached by the State Police in Houlton, had been looking at beaver activity along the Dole Pond road only miles away, and arrived soon after Simone got back to the camp. The crisp man who descended from the big Maine Department of Inland Fisheries and Wildlife truck brought some measure of order into the prevailing sense of panic, but Simone's memory of the day had only one clear picture: Mattie, wedged into a sofa corner in a tight fetal position, long arms wrapped around his knees and his head buried between them. As the realization of what had happened became undeniable to him, he had first wanted to race up the road to where his friend lay. Warned of the need to leave the site of the accident undisturbed, Serge and Gilles had stopped him, hanging onto him until he was quiet. At that point he had headed for the sofa and remained there, rocking rhythmically and occasionally humming a low, broken note.

Simone sat with him. She knew that talk was useless, but she hoped that he knew why she was there. She was glad that she wasn't part of the action outside. The snow had increased, hampering the whole business of recovering Jean-Yves's body. Gilles had taken the warden to find him, and when they eventually returned it was to report that he was satisfied that the death was an accident. A broken tree had brought a line-tensioner cable down and speed, poor visibility, and terrible timing had produced the fatal result. While time slowed to a painful crawl, the calm warden worked his way through the protocols for dealing with accidental, unattended deaths. Permission to move, and then release, the body had to be obtained from state authorities, and arrangements made to get Jean-Yves back to his family. The huddle of wet men in the sugar house seemed not to need her, beyond supplying hot coffee and the remains of Marie-Noëlle's pie, and she stayed, thankfully numb, in another sofa corner.

Meanwhile, Mattie rocked silently, out of reach of anyone. At some point, Serge had come into the cabin and now he sat, wet and sad, beside Simone.

"*Sacrement,*" he allowed himself. He gestured toward the sap house, where the warden was making calls with apparent ease.

"His phone outranks this thing," he said, waving his cell phone as if to try to catch a fleeting signal. "He called Marie-Noëlle. She's coming to get Mattie." He peered at his watch.

"Thank God the border is open late—she'll have to hustle though."

Hustling was something Marie-Noëlle had always been good at, and with time to spare she had braved the snowy roads and made it to the camp. She had taken her silent grandson, and sometime later the game warden had departed. He would be back the next day, he announced, and would supervise the removal of the body to the border.

* * *

The following morning brought no relief from the misery of the day before. Simone was the first up, and found herself making coffee and wondering what the hell was going to happen next. For starters, there was the aftermath of yesterday's disaster to be reckoned with. Jean-Yves, still in his snow suit, was in the equipment bay, resting on the trailer that had brought him out of the woods. She hoped she would be able to avoid going in there until the game warden had come to take him to the border and his awaiting family. Her only hope of surviving that whole tragedy was to let a third party deal with it. Her stomach lurched when efforts to avoid the memory of his contorted body in the snow failed her. She focused instead on a different, practical problem.

The weather had cleared and all signs were for a big sap flow. Did this mean Serge would have to make syrup? He had tap leases to pay, she reflected. The big block of maple producers in northern Somerset County operate under anomalous conditions. Rather than own their sugar bushes, they lease trees, paying a per-tap rate to the land management companies that operate the woods businesses for their distant corporate owners. Word along the Golden Road that year was that a hike in lease rates was planned. The hot-money hedge-fund creeps who pulled the strings from some distant city were squeezing the turnip for all the blood they could extract. In a good year, if yields were high and prices did not fall, the best producers made decent money, but nobody could afford to let a good sap run go uncollected.

Jean-Yves's family would be arranging a full Catholic ceremony, and soon, and Serge at least would need to be there. And what of Mattie? Marie-Noëlle would need some help in dealing with the traumatized boy. Putting it all together, Simone could feel the immediate future slipping out of her grasp. Serge was going to need help. She would make coffee and hope that Gilles would rise to the occasion and offer appropriate support. Then she would make her way to the border and call Linda. The thought of making contact with someone not mired in the catastrophe of the day before was a welcome one, and leaving a note for the still-sleeping guys she filled her travel mug with new coffee and drove to the border station.

She knew that she had been hoping to find Steve Haskell there, and was not ready for her disappointment when she found his backup officer, a sandy-haired, middle-aged woman who seemed unmoved by whatever she had heard. Simone muttered something about making phone calls, and realizing that she had no reason to be in the building to connect her phone, was headed back out when the woman asked, "Are you Simone?"

A tart "Why do you ask?" from Simone was cut short when she saw the officer holding out a sealed envelope with her name on it. She nodded an approximation of thanks and closed herself into the safety of her truck cab before opening it. It was a card with a picture of a bull moose, and inside, in well-formed handwriting, was the note:

I am so sorry about what happened to you all yesterday. I hope you are okay. I am away till tomorrow evening. See you when I get back? Steve Haskell.

A small gap in the clouds opened for a brief moment, and the feeling that despair was the only emotion she would ever feel lifted for a second. Buoyed by the thought, she dialed Linda at MOMP and found further relief by spilling the whole horrible story to her rational, listening friend and boss. There was business to do—Robert's scheduled inspection of Serge's and the LePage camps, and Simone's lingering reports from two days ago had to be addressed. The consideration of practical matters unrelated to death and tragedy brought the world back, briefly, into some sort of reasonable perspective. Simone ended the call by begging for a few days to get the situation and Serge's camp back to some sort of normalcy, and got the expected assurance from MOMP that she should take what time she needed. This would not be the first time that inspection reports had come in a few days after the event.

Before she started back to the camp, she took Steve's note out of the envelope and read it again. Fancy him having moose note cards at the ready. The sandy-haired B-team lady did not look like the animal note card type, so they must be his. And she liked the question mark at the end. It seemed to leave room for her to accept an offer rather than an expectation or a command.

The guys were up and caffeinated when she found them. Decisions had, apparently, been made, and Serge was running a short seminar on the monitoring of pumps.

"I'm good here for a few days," Simone offered, giving in to the inevitability of the moment.

* * *

Days passed—it could have been four or twice that many, as the only thing they kept track of was sap volume, vacuum pressure, and the barrel count of finished syrup. For the whole dreadful day that now seemed to have ended a life that she feared she would never see again, sap had run into holding tanks and then out through overflow lines into the snowbanks outside the camp. Once they got back to work, concentrating, boiling, filtering, and eventually sealing what the reservoirs had held into barrels of finished syrup had meant a twenty-four hour shift for all three Thibodeaus, followed by days of relentless work and inadequate rest. Simone felt like she was living in a tight, narrow tunnel and could see light only if she focused intently down the tube, ignoring everything and everyone that was not directly concerned with getting this damned unstoppable liquid into the barrels and out to the storage trailer. But they had done it. By the end of that spell of perfect sap flow weather, the trailer was half full of carefully labeled barrels.

Looking back, Simone realized that work was not all they had done. Food appeared from neighbors—she had a memory of anxious fellow maple producers, themselves stretched thin by the demands of the sap run, delivering the inevitable frozen pizzas and boxes of cookies. She had promised to be in touch with Steve Haskell but the memory of her emotional state on the day of Jean-Yves's accident embarrassed her. There had been a moment that felt dangerously personal and a line had come perilously close to being crossed. She felt no need to go back there, and managed to find reasons every day for staying in the camp and letting one of the guys make the occasional trip to the border, where their cell phones worked. One day, after she knew he was back at his post, she sent a note via Serge. After multiple abandoned attempts, all of which sounded cheesy or pathetic after she read them, she settled on *Thanks. Sorry I was such a mess,* which, while on the curt side of polite, was at least a step back from emotional and needy.

Concern over Mattie kept Serge in regular contact with home. Marie-Noëlle, who had raised the boy from the time his mother abandoned the family and his father moved to a city job in Montreal, reported that he hadn't moved from the state he had reverted to—rocking constantly with his head between his knees, refusing to talk. She hoped that time in the familiar house, where he had come through previous bouts of complete withdrawal, would eventually bring about his emergence from this stricken state. Out of other good options, they left his grandmother to care for him while they tried to salvage the sugar season.

And that was what they had done. The weather stayed fine: cold nights and warm, damp, still days. Under the pressure created by the endlessly flowing sap, a peculiarly satisfying pact was reached. Snow kept falling in small but steady increments, but Simone, Gilles, and Serge never got beyond the camp itself to check on lines or the pump house. They worked, ate, and slept and kept talk down to only what was needed to get the job done. Simone had to admit to herself that, as a team, they weren't all bad. Her father was uncharacteristically willing to take orders from his older brother, who in turn appeared to appreciate not only the work but the company of his estranged sibling. Simone was aware that she was the originator of the only abrasive moments, when she officiously reminded her elders of the need to keep written production records. Only after they had taken to addressing her as *Mlle l'Inspectrice* did she realize what a pain she was being, and that they didn't need reminding that she was a qualified professional and no longer the nuisance kid.

After however many days the sap run lasted, the weather turned colder and windy and the sap flow slowed. The two guys finally allowed themselves a couple of beers, and had passed out on the sofas, their sticky boots propped on milk crates. Word had come from MOMP that Robert was on his way to finish the two remaining inspections. Craving a change of scene, Simone announced a need for a hot bath, a real meal, and time to get the overdue reports to Linda. She wanted to retreat to the familiar comfort of Marie-Noëlle's home in Saint-Prosper, where she would get a night or two of good sleep and a chance to check up on Mattie. The guys could finish the last pans of syrup, clean up the camp, and cope with Robert's inspection. She was done, and getting out.

Steve was at his post at the crossing. He approached as her truck drove slowly over the icy expanse around the government buildings, and she was obliged to roll down her windows and meet his friendly gaze. Apparently uncertain of the reception any personal overtures might receive, he went with a simple "Everything going okay?" His diffidence and respect for boundaries prompted a warm response from Simone.

"Thanks. It's been tough, but we got a lot of syrup made. I'm going to check in on Mattie and get some desk work done. Then I can beat it back to my own place. Never thought I would be glad to get out of the woods, but this has been pretty awful."

She was slipping the truck into gear and winding up the window when she thought to add, "I've promised myself a drive home down the Golden Road, so I'll be back in a couple of days."

"Okay. I'll see you then. Take care. Get some rest."

Nice guy, she thought to herself again.

* * *

Left to themselves, the two men awoke the next morning to find themselves in a cold camp surrounded by piles of dirty clothes and empty pizza boxes. They struggled out of their beer-and-fatigue induced torpor. The fire was dead and the place strangely quiet. The big generator and the pumps and filters that it powered had been shut off before Serge and Gilles crashed, and with no equipment running the only sound was made by the wind, which had kicked up to a stiff breeze with tree-threatening gusts.

Gilles was first on his feet. He nudged his semiconscious brother with the toe of one boot.

"*Debout*," he commanded. "You want some breakfast? What time is it, anyway?"

"Uh, '*sais pas*—we shut it all down around three this morning. Have we even got anything worth eating here?"

A deep dive into the supplies—stuff that lingered in boxes dropped off by concerned neighbors—revealed a carton of eggs, a still-useable loaf of bread, and plenty of the inevitable coffee. The habits of the last few days had not yet worn off, and the two brothers swung into action without the need for discussion. With a fire in the stove, the small camp generator running, the first load of laundry churning in the old washer, and clean dishes drying in the rack, they consumed scrambled eggs and toast and felt the possibility of facing the next day.

A neat pile of folders had been placed on a separate card table that was free from the clutter that had filled the camp. A large sticky note on the top file read: *This is for Robert. Should be all he needs. I'll be back in a couple days. S.*

"*Merde.* The MOMP guy is coming today." Serge was used to having his affairs in order, and was aware that for the last few days he had relied entirely on Simone to maintain the necessary production logs. He pushed his empty plate aside and moved the files to the table. The pre-printed record sheets, tracking the dates and numbers of barrels filled, the R/O and big pan cleanings logs, plus the tapping records—by day, line, and tap count—from the weeks before sap had started to run, were all present and correct. Last year's final production tally and the pickup records, from the huge processor in New Hampshire who bought most of the bulk syrup produced along the Golden Road, were neatly clipped together, and the records binder held an envelope of receipts for supplies and equipment, including the all-important organically certified de-foamer oil receipt.

"Saved by your daughter," Serge remarked. "She's a good one. You know that, right?"

His brother's awkward relationship with his daughter annoyed Serge. The fool never seemed willing to admit that his behavior when she was little had anything to do with her prickly and defensive approach to the world. In Serge's mind, the problem was all part of Gilles's idiotic attitude toward women. The man can't handle the idea of independent, capable women, he reckoned. Simone's mother had given up on the effort to make a marriage based on shared strengths work, and the string of younger, awe-struck girlfriends that had overlapped with and followed that relationship had left Serge grateful for the friendship he shared with Marie-Noëlle and glad to stay away from the mess Gilles had made. His respect and affection for Simone had developed from the days she had skipped school to help him tap trees, and he wondered whether his brother would ever come to appreciate her.

"I do," was the surprising response. "Hadn't realized how much she knows about this stuff." Gilles motioned toward the stack of records. "I thought she just came up here to get away from me."

"It's not all about you, *tu sais*," Serge pointed out. "She believes in this life, you know. She's not afraid of real work."

The last comment scratched at old wounds. Serge had always disparaged what he saw as the soft life of a tenured academic, just as Gilles had scoffed at his choice to stay tired and dirty in the woods. The possibility of these old issues resurfacing was mercifully terminated by the arrival of a big SUV in the camp yard. Robert, the MOMP guy, resplendent in a huge rental vehicle, was climbing out of the thing, clutching files and measuring tapes.

"Oh shit," Serge said, checking his watch. "Poor guy said he would be here this morning and its already past noon. He's going to want to get across the border. Clear off the table, and I'll go get him."

"Come on in, it's warm in here," he said to the inspector, who shuffled across the ice and into the camp. He interrupted Serge's apologies.

"No problem," he assured them. "I came by this morning and couldn't find anyone up so I reversed things and did LePage first—he was getting ready to leave so he was happy."

"Ah, good. How are they doing?" Serge was torn between wanting to avoid all mention of his much-despised neighbors and curiosity about their operation.

"Pretty good," was Robert's cautious response. Aware of the friction between the two camps, and curtailed by strict rules of confidentiality, he wanted to stay away from revealing anything meaningful, but in the interest of friendly communication a general comment on the season seemed allowable.

"Seems like you guys had a good early run," he offered. "They were happy with it."

"Early run?" Serge asked. "We had a miserable start to the season. It wasn't until this last week that we made any decent amount of syrup."

To avoid getting any deeper into another client's production issues, Robert steered the conversation back to the Thibodeau camp. He offered condolences for the dreadful accident that everyone along the Golden Road was talking about, and made noises about getting the inspection done before the border closed. He needed to see the distant pump station, a trip to it having been abandoned during the last inspection. Last year's report contained some language about snowmobiles that wouldn't start, which Robert read as a reaction to weather and trail conditions too horrible for that year's inspection team to wrestle with.

Leaving the tour of the camp and review of records for later, Serge loaded the young man onto the Polaris and headed up the trail to the pump house. Anxiety made his heart pound. Neither he nor Gilles had ventured there since the day of the accident. Rounding the corner at the top of the rise, he was appalled by the sight of Jean-Yves's broken speedster still lopsidedly propped against the tree it had crashed into. The cable that had killed the boy was now mostly buried under the fresh snow from the past few days, and the tree that had once anchored it at a safe height was lying broken, as reported by the game warden.

Hoping to avoid any reference to this awful scene, he slowed the snowmobile and crept cautiously over the buried cable. Robert maintained a professional cool, saying nothing until they reached the pump house. Serge was impressed to find that everything there was in order. The pump house equipment had continued to run efficiently in the absence of anyone with time to carry out the usual checks.

Once Robert's quick inspection was done, he addressed a question to Serge.

"The LePage trees come up this ridge, right?" His maps showed the layout of the adjacent sugar bushes: the LePage trees below the trail and Serge's trees extending to the top of the ridge and along it beyond the pump house.

Serge pointed down the slope to where the drooping lines of the LePage operation could be seen.

"That's right. They go along the low rise all the way to the border," he confirmed.

"Mind if I take a minute to go look at their lines?" Robert asked. "The one guy at the camp didn't seem too keen on taking me up here. Won't take me long."

He's looking for undersized trees, Serge reckoned, thinking he'd likely find them too. As the inspector slithered over the icy crust that overlaid the snow pack, Serge looked back toward the scene of the accident.

That the kid rode recklessly was well known. He would have come around the corner and, anticipating a chance to fly up the straight track, would have gunned his racing machine for maximum speed. In the poor light of that dreadful day, the low-lying cable would have been invisible. The report had noted the broken anchor tree, and had judged the death accidental—yet another consequence of careless snowmobile operation.

Robert reappeared from his foray into the LePage trees, checking his watch and pointing out that he was running close to his deadline and still needed to see the camp and records. One thing at a time, Serge told himself. Get this guy on the road, see what Gilles's plans are, get him to help me retrieve that wretched snowmobile, figure out whether to call it on the sugar season, and, above all, get a full night's sleep.

Getting Robert on his way was easy. He made rueful and appreciative comments about Simone's inspection-ready records (apparently, others find her a bit over the top in attention to detail, Gilles noted with some satisfaction), recorded the production to date plus the final tallies from the previous year, and made it back to his awaiting chariot in time to get to Saint-Georges in daylight.

Serge turned to his brother.

"You in a rush to get out of here?" he asked, keeping any suggestion of which way he hoped the answer would go out of his question.

"Not really. Too tired. What's next here, anyway?" Gilles asked.

"I want to wrap this up and get home. Weather forecast is for full sun and temperatures going up into the teens—that's the 50s for you," Serge said. "That will shut off the season and we could pull taps and get out in a couple days. Plus that snowmobile is still halfway up a tree," he added. "We should go get it while there's enough snow on the ground to run a sled up there. Could use your help," was his simple request.

His direct plea appeared to have generated a coughing fit in Gilles. He cleared his throat and was evidently trying to say something.

"We could use some better food," was his first attempt at speech, followed by what was developing into an offer to call a friend and have her come in with a meal.

"You got a friend who would bring us food?" Serge was interested. "Who are you conning these days?"

"It's not like that. She's our age," Gilles addressed the first and most obvious source of Serge's disapproval. "We've been friends for a while— she's Bob LaVerdière's ex." He referenced a now-departed acquaintance from times when Serge used to hunt with Gilles and his Jackman friends.

"I could call her—she'd like it here. If she brought us some groceries I could stay and help you finish up. I should wait to see Simone, anyway—

she says she's going home down the Golden Road, so I wouldn't see her in Jackman."

"So go call. We are down to a can of beans and the rest of that bread. You might mention the shortage of beer here too."

The prospect of food and some ongoing help—not to mention his curiosity to see who his brother had hooked up with now—looked good to Serge. Anything that would get the season wrapped up and him back home. It would be a long time before being at the camp would be anything but a reminder of the guilt and grief he felt over Jean-Yves's death. He knew that trees could break and boys would ride dangerously, but if he had not left the pump-house chores to the boys, if he had checked lines or forbidden the use of that stupid racing machine, the kid would be alive today. Now that there was time to stop and think, he knew that he would forever feel that the accident had been his fault.

Still, working with Gilles had been good: shades of their youth, before their lives took such different paths.

Armed with his cell phone, Gilles was off to the border to call the hoped-for source of good food. Serge pulled damp laundry out of the washer and draped it around the fire. Life had to go on.

* * *

The town of Saint-Prosper lies a short fourteen kilometers from the border crossing at Saint-Zacharie. Simone parked her truck in the well-shoveled yard of Serge and Marie-Noëlle's house, pulling in beside the framed tent-cum-garage that was erected every winter to protect Marie-Noëlle's Forester and to save her the chore of scraping snow every time she wanted to use it. Simone felt no need to announce her arrival. This had been her second home for much of her adolescence, and a call had alerted her aunt that she planned to seek refuge and comfort there for a day or two.

The cozy house was full of the smell of something baking. This was all so unlike the other places she had grown up in—her father's series of rented pads that had never felt like her home and her mother's Spartan fixer-upper that she had been renovating ever since the divorce. The interior benefited from Marie-Noëlle's decorative talents. Embroidered linens, crocheted cushion covers, and knitted throws—things she had found time to make even while holding down a job at the library and raising first her own family and then her grandson—added to the homey comfort.

Simone found her aunt working in the kitchen on whatever it was that smelled so good. The usual kisses and concerns were exchanged, and Simone glanced into the living room at the curled-up form on the sofa. Mattie was working a game on his phone, shut off from the rest of the world. Marie-Noëlle caught Simone's eye and shook her head, adding a gesture of hopelessness as Simone dropped coat and hat onto a chair and approached Mattie. She sat carefully at the opposite end of the sofa, but he pulled his feet closer to himself and failed to take his eyes off his phone.

"It's okay," she tried to reassure him. "Just came to say Hi. I'm going for a shower."

She left him in his bubble. She followed a long shower with a nap, and emerged to find dinner on the table and Mattie surprisingly present and ready to eat. His nonverbal state made conversation around him painful, and any topic relating to the camp and the past days obviously impossible. Discussion of the weather and Simone's uncertain plans for the summer were all they could manage to talk about, and it wasn't long before all three had retired to their beds.

A day later, communication with Mattie had not changed. Simone had never known him to be this withdrawn. His grandmother insisted that he needed time before anything else was attempted. She would keep him safe and loved and wait for him to find, at least, a voice. Simone tried, but even making eye contact seemed too much for him. She had been one of the people he could talk to, but he was beyond even her reach. A thought occurred to her, and she sat beside him and tried touching his shoulder. He recoiled, but she kept a hand on him as she said: "It wasn't your fault, you know. It was an accident. That tree must have broken in the storm the night before. No way he could have known."

Her overtures were met with a shaking head and sort of low grunt of dissent. Too much for me, she recognized. Marie-Noëlle would give him some more time, and then maybe try going back to the therapists that had been some help in the past.

* * *

Two nights of comfort and care and her reports safely filed, she was ready to move on and get back to her own life. She would hit the sugar camp and make sure she wasn't needed anymore, then head back south.

As the US border shack came into view, Simone was determined not to look too anxious to see if Steve was back at his post. She had her passport at the ready and a business-like set to her shoulders as she entered the building. He was at his usual station behind the counter, but instead of taking her passport, he produced a sheepish grin and asked if she had a moment to spare. Fearing some sort of new information on Jean-Yves's death, she grunted "sure," and watched in some confusion as he reached behind the door to the small private office behind him and extracted an over-sized cat carrier in bright blue plastic, which he set on the counter in front of Simone. Without saying a word, he opened the front grill and motioned to Simone to look inside. What she saw, a plump gray form, could have been the result of a frog getting together with a pig. Whatever it was, the creature had a huge, gaping, anxious smile and a skinny tail with a white tip that quivered uncertainly against its fat stomach.

Simone took her eyes away from the pale blue gaze from inside the crate, and looked up at Steve, who was nervously monitoring her reaction.

"My sister," he started to explain. Surely he wasn't claiming that thing as his sister, Simone thought, but he stumbled on.

"She got a rescue dog from some outfit in New York and didn't know it was pregnant. She had this one puppy and Julie has her hands full and I promised to take care of her. I'm sort of fostering her, but I can't have a dog here. She needs a home." There was a long pause while they both looked at the grinning pup, now beginning to squirm against the back of the carrier in anticipation of being pulled out.

"I—I thought you might like her." Steve ended his explanation on a lame note, evidently aware that he had stepped onto dangerous ground. To fill the dead space left in the air, he reached in and extracted the fat puppy, which could now be identified as a half-grown pit bull, whose tail was wiggling for its full length.

Not knowing what else to do, Simone accepted the wriggling being and was obliged to clamp it against her chest to avoid dropping it. As soon as the pup was in her arms, it righted itself to face her, gave a gigantic heave of its rotund form, and managed to get both front paws around her neck. Before she could react, the puppy was energetically licking her ear, and to her great embarrassment, Simone found herself weeping into the soft, fat wrinkles of the dog's neck.

"Oh my God, I am so sorry," Steve reached for the puppy, horrified by the reaction and wanting to right the boat to a more stable and impersonal level. But instead of handing the dog back, Simone held on, unable to look up or to stop crying. Taking a different tack, Steve, for the second time in their acquaintance, found himself steering an emotional Simone into a chair, while she fished a wad of paper towel out of a pocket and made an effort to regain a measure of dignity.

"I can't have a dog either," she told him, once speech was restored. "I can't look after one." By now the pup had collapsed comfortably against her and was attempting to get her hair out its enormous mouth. She pulled it back onto the center of her lap and took a long look. It was a mid-sized, female, adolescent, fat-headed street pit and its blue eyes, fixed directly and purposefully on Simone's, said only one thing: *you cannot win this one.*

Steve Haskell sensed the moment and took immediate advantage.

"Maybe you could just take her while you are here?" he suggested. "She'll be much happier at your camp than stuck here with me. Julie says she is all good to go—house broken, shots, everything. You can bring her back when you have to leave."

Still not sure of her voice, and definitely not knowing how to respond to the man and his perfect gift and timing, Simone mumbled a series of okays and tried to stuff the animal back into its crate. It was soon clear the pup had a very different idea, and taking the path of least resistance, Simone sat her on the passenger seat while Steve appeared with a disconcertingly ready-to-go armful of dog bed, bowls, food, and leashes, which he dropped into the truck bed before coming round to Simone's window.

"She needs a name," he said. "Julie just called her Baby Girl."

"Okay," Simone replied—which seemed to be her entire vocabulary for now.

Alone with the pup for the short drive to camp, she looked at her eyes, which maintained their lock on her face, and thought, blue eyes, Blue Ivy. "You are Ivy," she said to the gargoyle beside her. "Now stay on your side of the truck." Ivy opened her mouth to let a vast pink tongue fall out, and without seeming to use her legs, oozed from the passenger seat and into Simone's lap, awkwardly entwined with the gear shift and the coffee travel mug. *J'y suis, j'y reste* was the message, and Simone decided she wasn't in the mood to argue.

* * *

A small Honda with Maine plates was parked in the yard when Simone and Ivy arrived back at the sugar camp. Simone dropped the reluctant dog onto the mud and grabbed her backpack.

"You want to get warm, you'll have to follow me," she explained to Ivy. They pushed the door open and entered the camp together, Ivy's instinct for survival and her determination to keep Simone in sight at all times needing no further guidance. Simone made a quick assessment of the scene. The camp was tidy, and a bed had been made up on one of the sofas. The explanation for this came through the door from the sugar house, clutching a jug of fresh syrup.

"Jocelyne—what the hell brought you up here?" Simone asked.

"Hey, good to see you too. And what on earth is that?" Jocelyne put the syrup on the table and went to embrace Simone. They both looked at Ivy, who was completing a tour of the camp and homing in on the woodstove.

"Um, that's Ivy." Simone realized that explaining Steve, and why a border officer had given her a puppy, was going to be complicated, so she went back to her question.

"They sounded a bit desperate," was Jocelyne's explanation. "I've heard so much about this place and I didn't mind an excuse to come visit. Seemed like a good idea—and I hadn't seen Serge in years."

Simone looked around. Her unspoken question was answered by Jocelyne.

"They've gone to get Jean-Yves's snowmobile. I think they were putting it off, but they had to move while they could still get up there." They all knew that with the predicted rise in temperatures, the trails would become unusable by any vehicle.

"I was about to fix them something. They took off without breakfast before the road gets too soft."

"Nice of you. I thought you and he…?" Simone's question trailed off.

"Yeah, I know. He can be an ass. But he seems happier up here and I'm glad he's getting together with Serge. Might do him some good. And anyway…" Jocelyne gestured toward the bed on the sofa.

"Keeping it simple," she said.

Simone reflected briefly on the conversation she'd had with her father all those days ago. If that was the cause of Jocelyn's concern over his mood, then "keeping it simple" was an obvious way to avoid sources of trouble. Anyway, it all felt like a whole life ago, before a far sadder event had taken over their existence.

* * *

Up on the hill the Thibodeau brothers had disentangled the broken machine from the tree and were pausing to consider how they were going to get it onto the big equipment sled they had towed up. Leaning against the Polaris, Gilles surveyed the slope below them.

"Those asshole LePages run a truly crappy operation," he commented, looking at the old sap lines and the untended sugar bush. Careful producers keep dead trees and competing evergreens away from their lines, but the LePage woods showed little sign that anyone had practiced any kind of management for many years.

"No shit. Can't imagine how they make a dime, but the inspector fellow seemed to think they were doing okay. The trees by their camp must be in better shape," Serge offered.

A thought occurred to Gilles.

"You know anything about what the rest of the family is up to?" he asked. He recounted in some detail the episode with the Hummer.

"Where they getting the money to run a fancy piece of shit like that?" he added.

"Not from this outfit," his brother responded. "These boys are the two loser nephews. It's their uncle Benoit who has all the money. He has a trucking business, but word around town is he's found his way into the drug market. Supplemental income!"

"Well, I hope to hell he gets caught and strung up." In the spirit of the improved communication that had developed between them, Gilles offered a short version of his experience buying bootleg pills from one of the LePages.

"Hmm—that stuff has gone open-market now. No money left in it," Serge remarked. "Why do you care anyway? You can get it cheap in the States now. You don't even need these bastards."

"I know, but it was easy and I didn't have to let the whole of Jackman know what I was buying," Gilles confessed. The small town grapevine would have been unable to keep that secret.

"What the hell is he selling now?" he wondered.

"They say that there's a lot of harder stuff moving across the border." Serge's local connections had been talking. "Used to be just out west, but it's catching on here too. This border is pretty porous, I guess."

It was not lost on either of them that they were standing less than a kilometer from the Canadian line, with nothing to mark it in places but a few strands of barbed wire or a clear cut strip through the woods.

"Hmm. Nothing those jerks do would surprise me." Serge's fervent desire to have nothing to do with his neighbors or any of their family, coupled with the fact that the day was warming and the snow getting sticky, got them back to their task. They wrestled the crumpled Arctic Cat onto the sled and, finding no reason to linger in this depressing spot, set off down the hill.

Over sausages and pancakes and another round of coffee, a plan to deal with the end of the season was resolved. The warm weather was signaling an end to the sap flow. As soon as the snow pack was gone and maple buds developing, the sap would become "buddy" and off-flavor. Jocelyne and Gilles would stay to help finish up production, pull the taps from the trees, and close up the camp, and Simone could finally get back to her long-postponed plan to drive south, though this time with a companion, who would have to get used to the idea that she had to ride in the passenger seat.

Out in the yard she avoided the sled and its sad cargo, and chose a short loop around the closest trees for a pre-truck-ride pee run for Ivy.

The untraveled snow there was soft and wet, and Ivy rolled delightedly in a fresh patch that was blackened with a dense dusting of snow-fleas, the strange little springtails that cover the snow in late winter. Backing them up as sure signs of the coming spring thaw, fat cones of skunk cabbage were emerging in the wet spot at the foot of the maple ridge. The seasons change suddenly up here, Simone reflected. One day you are breaking through icy crust on the top of the winter's snow pack, and the next it is all turning to water and flushing out the rivers and roads as it heads to the sea. Time for her to head that way with Ivy, now that maple season was winding down.

Leaving the camp was unexpectedly difficult. The stress and the hard labor of the last couple of weeks had created a strange sense of shared survival. Finding no words that worked, she limited her acknowledgment of this new feeling to an awkward hug for her father and a warmer embrace for Serge.

"Sure you are okay?" she asked him. "I can stay and help pull taps if you need me." Both the organic standards and the rules set by the land management companies required all taps to be out of the trees within thirty days of the end of the season.

"Don't worry, we can handle it. Couple of days is all we need."

Cleared for take-off, Simone turned to Jocelyne.

"Stay cool, and make sure these bozos say thank you."

"Don't worry. I am counting on Serge for good manners, and I can always withhold food if they don't behave."

There was one more thing to do before she could finally get out of the woods. Steve Haskell was in his office when she and Ivy got there. In response to his questioning look, Simone risked a rueful smile.

"I guess I am going to need her papers," she said, as Ivy waggled her way to Steve's feet and rolled over to display a bulging pink belly for him to rub.

"I'm headed," Simone added, nodding at the truck.

"Where to?" Steve asked.

"I have a place in LaGrange, but I'm going to go check in with my mom in Liberty."

"Liberty? That's cool—right next to where I live." He paused, then carried on as an idea struck him. "I have two days off next week. If you're still there, maybe I could bring her papers over?"

Simone was taken off guard and had to fall back on another round of "okays."

"Text me," she said, writing a phone number on the note pad that sat on the desk. "I'll be there for a few days."

"I'll do that." He pocketed the slip of paper and gave the puppy another pat.

"Did you give her a name?" he asked

"Ivy," Simone said.

"Nice. Evergreen and clingy?"

"No, not clingy. Just firmly attached." This time Simone allowed herself a real smile. "Actually, she is perfect. Thank you. Really. She is just right."

The two of them set off down the Golden Road, Simone's anticipation of a solitary drive now greatly improved by the contented presence beside her.

4

Simone drove past the Welcome to Liberty—Home of Liberty Graphics sign with a certain feeling of entering a different state than the one she had just left. She never felt as comfortable in this part of Maine, the region just to the west of the rapidly gentrifying coastal towns of Belfast and Rockport and the country-club and yachting communities of Camden/Rockland. True, it offered more than mere survival, leading an uneven swing from rural poverty to rural renewal of a sort. She knew that the combination of the proximity to growing markets, reasonably good soils, and a relatively mild climate was probably what had attracted a population of new farmers, but she wondered whether it wasn't just the names of the small municipalities that form the western edge of Waldo and Knox counties—Unity, Union, Freedom, Liberty, Hope, and Friendship—that appealed to the homesteading, organic, back-to-the-landers that had moved into this area. Either way, the small revolution in rural living, one that Simone's mother became part of when she bought an abandoned farmhouse after her divorce from Gilles Thibodeau was final, was breathing new life into a once run-down part of the state.

Her mother had been offered the house as a tear-down, but rather than destroy a charming old home, she had been painstakingly restoring it over more than a decade. To Simone, years ago, it had felt like being forced to camp out in a rotting shell of a building. Friends with newer houses, with reliable heating systems and rat-free attics, had deemed the place unsuitable for sleepovers, and she had gone through high school with the stigma of living in a shabby home. But now she was obliged to admit that the effort had been worth it. Fixing the basement, roof, and windows had been the first priorities, none of which had had much effect on the amenities offered by the house. But new exterior clapboards plus maple floors and a real kitchen had resulted in an attractive and character-filled home, and she was ready to embrace the comforts of what, to her, was almost suburban living.

She drove cautiously up the rough drive. She did not expect to find her mother home. It had been her understanding that her mother considered her job of parenting to have ended when Simone left for college. She was conscious of a nagging resentment that her mother's life was so independent and, apparently, fulfilling. Friends of hers had parents who seemed to need constant contact with their children, with rituals of daily phone calls and family holidays. Simone was likely to call her mother and find she was embarking on some weird adventure—volunteering to monitor sea turtles in the Galapagos had been the latest one. Still, she was sure that her mom would love Ivy, and she hoped that she would earn some approval for having taken on the responsibility of a owning a dog.

Tess the border collie, who divided her time between Ellie James (Simone's mother had never relinquished her own name) and the next door neighbors, came tearing out from under the porch, suggesting that someone was home. Taking an extra turn with the leash around Ivy's thick neck, to ensure that she could not slip out of her collar, Simone opened the truck door and let the two girls meet each other. To her relief, Ivy ducked her head between her front paws and then turned upside down in full "beat me up but please love me" position. So much for fighting genes, thought Simone. Tess was yipping and dodging, inviting the recumbent form to get up and play. This evolved into a prolonged butt-sniffing event, and Simone left them to get acquainted as she made her way into the house.

Conversations with Ellie tended to focus on Simone's failure to find a regular job since leaving college and her mother's accounts of her trips and projects. This time, however, Simone had the better stories and found her mother to be a good listener for a change. Beyond concern for the effect it had had on her daughter, the death of a boy she had never met was not of great concern to her. A dozen or more people die every year in Maine from snowmobile accidents. Speed, alcohol, trees, and rough trails make for dangerous riding, and news of snowmobile fatalities rarely spreads beyond the local media. But Simone's report of her time with her father and uncle caught Ellie's attention. As the day ended and they settled down to share Ellie's customary night-cap of a glass of good bourbon, she recapped the conversation of the afternoon.

"So—you got to work with your dad? Sounds like that went okay?" she ventured.

Simone postponed further dissecting of the accident and events immediately following it and recounted the drive up to the sugar camp, leaving out the details of Gilles's anger at the LePages but mentioning Jocelyne and her apparent place in his life.

"I don't know why she bothers with him," she said, adding a question she had never asked before. "Come to think of it, why did you put up with him for so long?"

"Oh, you have no idea how much energy I wasted being made miserable by that man. I thought I was in love with him. It wasn't all his fault, you know. He was a shit, but I was a mess. Takes two to screw up a relationship, and I did my part."

This confession had the effect of irritating Simone. Now her mother was going to show off her state of complete mental robustness by "taking responsibility." A diatribe on forgiveness would probably follow.

"So why did you stay with him? I still had to live through years of you two fighting."

"Oh, God, I know. I am so sorry. I was such a long way from my family and had so many demons to deal with. It made me into a needy pain who clung to men who lied to me. Took a while to get up the courage to leave."

Ellie paused and took a long look at her daughter.

"You know, after I had you I didn't care anymore. I really just wanted to raise you to be happy and safe. I probably didn't do such a good job. Things were a bit rough here for a while, I guess."

She poured them each another small measure of whiskey before capping the bottle firmly and returning it to its shelf.

"Seriously. I do want you to be happy and not mad at your parents all the time. Your dad's not really a bad man, you know. Just a damaged, self-centered one that lots of women have loved, and not all for the wrong reasons. But believe it or not, I forgive him for it all."

Here it is, thought Simone. The saintly Ellie James. An exasperated grunt escaped her, and, sensing her daughter's discomfort, Ellie changed the subject.

"Now that maple season is over, what are your plans?" she asked.

This was more familiar territory for Simone, and she had a response ready.

"Back to the greenhouse for now," she said. The room she rented in LaGrange was attached to a busy greenhouse operation. Her landlady grew a robust crop of vegetable and flower seedlings and needed all the help available to get it sold in the brief Maine planting season. She was ready for her mother's next question with a poorly thought-out plan that she hoped would sound convincing.

"I've promised to help this spring, but I've been thinking about getting some more inspection qualifications. There's plenty of work for inspectors," she said. "I could take a fancy training course and then apply to work for the big certifiers."

Their brief consideration of Simone's future as a full-service organic farm inspector was interrupted by the two dogs, who despite an energetic afternoon were now engaged in a noisy game of ear-biting.

"That thing is going to have to learn some better behavior before it gets much bigger," Ellie commented, with a disapproving glance at Ivy.

"I know. I could use some help. Maybe I could hang here for a few days. We could do boot camp for Ivy, which is her name, by the way. She will be hell at the greenhouse if she doesn't learn some manners. Anyway, I need to be here for a couple of days. The guy I got her from lives in Albion. He said he would bring her papers over."

She hoped she could slide the mention of Steve into the conversation without generating a bunch of questions from Ellie. To her relief, her mother seemed sufficiently taken with the prospect of sharing her puppy-training techniques with Simone to let the reference to a guy go right past her.

* * *

The promised delivery of Ivy's records took place two days later. Out of uniform, Steve turned out to be the normal son of a local tractor dealer.

Needing an excuse to get away from Ellie, Simone used Ivy's need to practice walking to heel as an excuse for a walk. Ambling across the fields with the compliant dog made conversation easy. Steve described a predictable upbringing of high school boredom and hunting events with his father, followed by a spell in the military and his recent transformation into a Customs and Border Protection officer. The isolation of a tiny outpost on the northern Maine border did not bother him, he said. After being too close to too many guys in the army, he claimed that the quiet and relatively uneventful life in the Saint-Zacharie station suited him.

"I get that," Simone said. "My mom thinks I should want some real job, or grad school, or something, but I hate being around tons of people."

"You get up to the sugar camp any other part of the year?" Steve wanted to know, but Simone could come up with no reason to be back in either Jackman or the camp outside of syrup season. The unstated invitation hung in the air, neither of them able to think of a follow-up. The walk over, Steve prepared to leave.

"Write—or Skype me, or something?" he asked. "Keep me posted on Ivy's progress. Julie will want to see pictures."

A safe reason for staying in touch having been established, Simone watched him drive away. She managed to dodge Ellie's questions by bringing the evening conversation back to Gilles.

"I may go back up to Jackman for another visit after the greenhouse closes up," she told her mother. Ellie misread her motives and was back to the problems between Simone and her father.

"It wouldn't be a bad thing for you to be able to get past being so pissed off at your dad," she said.

"I'm not mad at him all the time," Simone had to admit, but an uncomfortable memory of his pill-buying confessions came back to her. "It's just that he can be such a dick. I mean seriously. But maybe he's figured something out with Jocelyne. She's not just another girlfriend—maybe."

From her lofty position of survivor-with-a-good-life, Ellie had words of wisdom to offer.

"I think your dad is just another guy afraid of growing old, and wanting to prove he's still got it. But like I say, it's not your problem to fix and you had no part in the making of it. You have your own life to figure out."

Figuring out the whole of life was too big a challenge for Simone to contemplate, but two days later, as she drove up the esker that runs north from Bangor to LaGrange, she was inclined to think that the immediate future looked better than it had a couple of weeks earlier. It wasn't until she was well past Bangor that she was willing to admit that finding an interesting guy in her life had turned a small light on somewhere in her consciousness.

* * *

Late winter became spring and spring was turning toward summer as Maine's brief, intense greenhouse season was slowing down. Six weeks of full-on tending a rapidly growing crop and impatient customers had peaked with a blow-out Memorial Day weekend. Simone's landlady and seasonal supplier of income was left with empty benches, a full cash register, and time to turn to her own garden. A big cleanup could wait while they all took a few days off.

For their part, Simone and Ivy had to look ahead to their next move. Communication with Serge and Gilles had been minimal, a situation that was not all their fault, she had to admit. A brief email from Marie-Noëlle had reported that Mattie was still jumpy and withdrawn, but was helping her shelve books in the library and was about to start seeing his therapist. Simone decided to risk a text message.

Hey Matts. She used the name she had called him when he was a little shadow who would follow her teenage self around the woods. *Thinking of you. Things OK?*

She was working on ways to override Ivy's total lack of impulse control when it came to squirrels, cats, or, for that matter, anything furry that moved, when her phone pinged. That didn't take long, she thought, seeing Mattie's name on her screen.

Ce n'était pas un accident, the message read. *Ils savaient que nous les avons vus.*

What the hell, she thought. What in the world does he mean? They knew we saw them? Who knew? Saw what?

What do you mean? Tell me, she wrote, but the communication stopped there. She repeated the message in French. He could read, write, and speak English but maybe this would get a response. She returned to Ivy's lessons and waited for more information, but her phone stayed silent.

Now what am I supposed to do? she asked herself. She trusted Mattie not to bullshit her, but one short text was not enough information to act on. And why was he telling her this, whatever it was? Giving up on getting anything else from him that day, and unnerved by the thought of what he was hinting at, she tried a call to Serge's phone. The call went straight to voice mail. Of course, she thought, he uses the thing only for emergencies. He probably doesn't have it turned on, if he even has it on him. She tried Marie-Noëlle's phone instead, which picked up immediately.

Not wanting to alarm her aunt over something she herself did not understand, she enquired simply about Mattie. No change, was the report. He was still mostly not talking and would leave the house only to go to the library with his grandmother. She was worried about him. He seemed to be stuck in the trauma of losing his one friend. And no, there was no way he would come to the phone.

"Where's Serge?" Simone wanted to know. "Can I have a word with him?"

New Hampshire was the answer. Word was that the big maple syrup wholesale buyer there might drop some of the smaller producers. Maple prices were down, influenced by a glut in Canadian production, and Serge was making a preemptive move, taking the trouble to go down and see the buyer in person, and remind his contact there of their long-standing relationship. The wholesaler's crew would be coming in to pick up syrup as soon as the roads were dry enough, and he was leaving nothing to chance.

The syrup pickup business was a sore subject with Simone. Put together all the producers in this piece of Maine and you have the biggest syrup-producing block in the country, but even so, nearly 100 percent of the added value derived from bottling and retailing this precious, natural sweetener went to processors in other states. She never got why Maine couldn't get its act together enough to keep some of that money in the state. Just another example of how little attention anyone paid to this amazing business hiding off the grid in the woods.

She reminded herself that Serge had a more immediate problem to deal with.

"So—can I come up for a quick visit?" Simone asked. Maybe Mattie would talk to her in person. She had to find out what the hell this was about, and besides, she could always run over to the border and let Steve check out Ivy's progress toward disciplined adulthood.

With the promise of the usual welcome and the assurance that she could be spared from the greenhouse until the next weekend, Simone headed out the following morning, up the familiar road to Jackman and the Canadian border.

Her cross-country route from LaGrange put her onto State Route 201N in Bingham. From there the road follows the Kennebec River to The Forks, where outfitters, fly-fishing guides, and rafting companies advertise their backwoods adventure options on the Kennebec and its fast-running tributary, the Dead River. It was still early for the rafting businesses to be at full operating level, but a few wet-suited white-water canoe and kayak parties could be seen at access points along the river. Leaving both rivers behind, the road winds through the mountains until it reaches Jackman. That dumb sign on Gilles's camp road is probably right, Simone reflected. It must be an easy seventy-five miles from the last traffic light in Skowhegan to the next—and only—light in Jackman.

Last time she had driven this route it had been late winter, with dirty snowbanks piled against shuttered buildings and a general air of dilapidation lying heavily over the roadside communities. But a sense of possibility had returned to the area with the onset of spring, and Simone was reminded that despite poverty and depression, this was still a beautiful place. The trees were still displaying all the color variations of new spring growth, and salt and dust-tolerant weeds were transforming the edges of the roads.

Her pleasure at being back in the bit of Maine where she felt most at home was clouded by the purpose behind her mission.

What in the world is Mattie talking about? she asked herself again. This had to have something to do with those blasted LePages. Her mind ran over the days before Jean-Yves's accident, and the conversation she had had with him and Mattie. When she had conveyed Linda's request for information to them, all she had wanted to know was whether the LePage camp was operating. That was easily accomplished without intruding into their operation. So what else had gone on? What had the two boys done, and what had they seen? Damn Mattie, she thought. Why is he telling me shit I don't understand, and what on earth does he think I can do about it?

She drove through Jackman, ignoring the twinge of guilt she felt about not stopping to see Gilles. With nothing more to go on than the brief emails she had exchanged with her family over the past weeks, she was anxious to get to Saint-Prosper and figure out some answers to Mattie's weird message. The Armstrong border station required a longer stop than usual, this being Ivy's first venture into Canada. The vaccination records that Steve had supplied were deemed in order and they were waved through, but Simone was taken aback by the warning from the agent that pit bulls were banned from the province of Ontario. Her grinning companion had attempted to lick the face off the officer as he looked into the truck and Simone had to suppress a series of smart remarks about Ontarians' problems with being kissed. She assured the agent that nothing would induce her to go near the place and that she was just on her way to Saint-Prosper and family.

When she reached the house, Mattie was alone and in his room with the door firmly shut. Knowing that it was useless to try breaching his defenses and frustrated by his inaccessibility, Simone took Ivy for a walk, hoping that when Marie-Noëlle came home Mattie would emerge— from his room, at least, if not from his silence and withdrawal. She ran her questions for Mattie through her mind again. What had the boys seen, and who had seen them? Was he suggesting that whatever he had seen had led to Jean-Yves's death? What did he mean about it not being an accident? Why for the love of God had Mattie waited until now to say anything? What did he think she could do about it?

The image of the yellow Hummer and her father's fury at the LePages kept coming back to her. She had overheard Serge and Gilles venting disgust at the whole family of LePages and speculating about their drug-derived wealth, but had never associated it with the two clowns who ran the maple operation. Could there really be something going on there that Mattie and Jean-Yves had seen?

She decided it was pointless to try to develop exotic theories about drug-running back-woodsmen until she knew more from Mattie, and hoped that he would recognize that her presence there was in response to his text, and talk to her. He owed her that much, she reasoned. But his door was still firmly shut when she got back to the house, and Marie-Noëlle had little to offer by way of suggestion on how to get him to communicate.

"He's never this bad," she confessed to Simone. "I can't tell what's going on with him. I mean, Jean-Yves dying like that was devastating. I understand that. But there's something else. It's like he's afraid to talk to anyone about what happened."

Well, that makes sense, thought Simone. If he is trying to tell me that something more than an accident caused Jean-Yves's death, he should be scared. Still, not wanting to turn unexplained suspicions into full-blown panic, she told her aunt about Ivy's origins and her plan to run over to the border in the morning to let the dog's adoption agent see the progress she was making.

Dinner provided no more opportunities to pry explanations out of Mattie. He avoided eye contact and was headed back to his room after the meal when Simone tried a new approach.

"Hey, come meet Ivy for real." She motioned to his corner of the sofa, which Ivy had been warming while they ate. "She needs to learn to be polite to new people." Clicking her fingers at Ivy, she got a grudging agreement to move partway down the sofa.

Evidently, talking to the dog presented less challenge to Mattie's communication issues than did talking to people, and he took up his corner position with little hesitation. Ivy shunted herself toward him and, showing unusual restraint, shoved herself against Mattie and dropped her fat head into his lap. With a comfortable wriggle that settled her curves against him, she looked as if she could stay there for the rest of time. Mattie pulled at her ears and she produced grunts and a subdued but grateful tail wag. God bless her, though Simone. That's the most comfortable I have seen him look since the accident.

Her desire to interrogate her cousin was quashed by the pleasure at seeing him relax with Ivy. There was a palpable lowering of tension in the boy and in the room. Don't spoil this moment, she told herself. But still, she had to know what it was he had hinted at, and as she felt the irritation at his silence return, she tried to introduce the subject. Marie-Noëlle was busy with something at the kitchen sink, and taking advantage of the cover this gave her, Simone reached out and rubbed Ivy's plump butt, catching Mattie's eye for a brief moment.

"What was it you saw?" she asked. "*Qu'est-qui çest passé?*"

She sensed a stiffening in Mattie's body, but she went on. "Tell me what you want me to do."

She fought to keep the frustration out of her voice, but she could feel that she was losing him. He was pushing Ivy's bulky mass off his lap and making for the safety of his bedroom. Simone took a step toward him and lowered her voice to the softest tone she could summon.

"Seriously, Matts," she said, "you have to give me a bit more than that."

He paused and seemed to struggle to respond to her. As he maneuvered his way past her he seemed to sense the urgency of her request and the fact that she was there, offering help. Almost in a whisper, but clearly, he managed to say:

"*Vas voir. Tu verras que j'ai raison.*" He paused to struggle again, this time making the effort to look directly at her. She was aware of a pleading, fearful expression on his face that quickly returned to the emotionless state that had become normal, and he was gone to the seclusion of his room.

Well, shit, she thought. What did he mean, *Go see and you'll see that I'm right?* That didn't help a lot. Now what? Ivy had reclaimed the corner of the sofa, but moved over at Simone's command. Simone let the dog scooch partway onto her lap and found comfort in twirling the dog's ears through her fingers as she considered her options. Mattie's dropped hints and evident plea for her involvement were impossible to ignore. That he had trusted her enough to share even this meager information was, she knew, a huge expression of confidence. His attention to detail and his inability to shade truth told her that he knew—or believed—that something bad had happened, and he trusted her to figure it out. How could she ignore that? But what could she do? One dropped hint and one sorrowful request to "go see," coupled with his assertion that she would then figure something out, were hardly enough to report foul play to any authorities. The scene had been examined and the death declared an accident. She couldn't change that without a good deal more information.

She had to be back at the greenhouse by the end of the next day. The weekend after Memorial Day was a big sale event, a chance to move the remaining stock out to new homes where it could turn into summer crops of flowers and vegetables, and she would be needed. But she had all of the next day, and there was obviously only one thing to do.

She gave Ivy a slap on her haunch, prompting a delighted wriggle.

"I guess it's you and me, Fatso," she confided to the dog. "We'll go see what the fuck the kid is talking about. You game?"

Ivy's unquestioning response was reassuring. They would stop by to see Steve, take a look around the LePage camp and the accident site, and then repeat the long drive down the Golden Road, making it back to LaGrange by evening. She assumed that Mattie was right. If she went to look, she would see what he was talking about, and then she could decide what to do next.

* * *

Simone drove slowly toward Saint-Zacharie the next morning. The small farms along the road were gradually turning from brown mud patches to green fields. The winter livestock pens still provided the only dry standing, but the fields would soon offer relief. Ice fishing shacks had been pulled off the lakes, and only the cold north shores still held any remnant frozen patches. Spring was forcing its way in, even here. She remarked, for the hundredth time in her life, the contrast between this settled, busy, small-town life on the Canadian side of the border and the barely inhabited wilderness on the Maine side.

As she approached the border station, Simone was conscious of some fear that Steve would not be happy to see her. The plan they had made in Liberty to keep in touch via Skype had not gone well. Simone found video calls awkward and oddly invasive, and her discomfort had led to an early abandonment of the plan. She blamed herself for the failure to find a replacement means of communication. She had let a couple of friendly text messages from Steve go unanswered, and he had apparently given up on the effort. Now she felt regret and embarrassment in anticipation of finding him at his post. Stupid bitch, she said out loud, hastening to reassure Ivy that she meant herself and not the amiable dog. You coulda tried a little harder—poor guy is only trying to be a friend. She had, however, managed to type a short text that morning, announcing her plan to come through the crossing on her way home down the Golden Road.

She found Steve to be his predictable, unruffled self, amused by her mumbled apologies and references to a busy season in the greenhouse and poor cell-phone reception in LaGrange. He was too busy fending off Ivy's wet and effusive greetings to do more than usher them into the building for the routine check of papers. Simone sought refuge in the customary seclusion of the bathroom, where she once again had to admit to herself that this was truly a nice, normal, uncomplicated man who deserved something better than a brush-off from her. He was, after all, the supplier of her now firmly established best friend and companion. She came back into the office resolved to be nicer, and found Steve feeding Ivy the remains of a breakfast burrito of uncertain origins. Ivy seemed determined to prove that her lessons in citizenship were paying off, and had assumed an awkward squat that was almost a regulation "sit" but that left room for a quick leap in case the burrito needed catching. Not wanting to be left out, Simone let Steve compliment her on Ivy's progress.

She could find no way to explain her mission that did not sound foolish or alarmist. In response to his official question about her stay in Canada, she merely reported a quick visit to Saint-Prosper. She checked with him on activity at the sugar camps and was assured that nobody had been in since the season ended.

"Braisethwaites and the Sugar Shack people will be coming in soon," he informed her, naming the two big buyers of bulk syrup. "Roads are drying up now and they'll be able to get trucks in if this keeps up." He made a vague gesture skywards, where sun and a breeze were indeed creating ideal drying conditions. Nice weather overhead did not automatically translate into good going underfoot, but with another week of fine weather dust would be more of a problem than mud on the unpaved roads.

"Thought you'd be glad to see how the mutt is coming along," Simone said. "She's almost full grown now—just needs a year or two for her brain to catch up." Ivy's furiously wagging tail signaled her complete agreement with anything Simone said.

"I knew you two would get along." Steve sounded pleased with the success of his matchmaking. "She's going to be twice the size of her mother, but she sure is cute."

That anyone could describe Ivy as cute made Simone laugh. As she opened the passenger-side door for Ivy to haul herself into the truck, she admitted to Steve that this was the best present she had ever been given.

"You're welcome," he responded. "Glad it's working out. Drive safe. They are starting to move logs again, so watch out for trucks."

Serge's camp had a shut-down, resting air when Simone and Ivy arrived in its yard. She retrieved the key from its hiding place under a brick in the old outhouse and let herself into the camp. She was glad to find it tidy and clean. For good measure, she checked in the old shipping trailer Serge used for storage, and found the full barrels of syrup lined up in orderly rows waiting for collection. With no clear idea of what she should do to verify Mattie's suspicions, unsure of what she was looking for or what she might find, she looked around for an excuse to delay her mission, but with no generator running and the propane shut off, even a cup of coffee would be a hassle to make. Not worth it, she decided. The obvious thing to do was to hike up the road to the pump house and find the spot where Jean-Yves and his machine had come to grief. Despite her doubts that she would find anything conclusive, her sense of loyalty to Mattie was compelling her to try.

"Come on, lazybones," she commanded Ivy, who had taken up a hopeful position next to the cold wood stove. "Let's go see what we can see."

She admitted to herself that the dog was welcome company. Ivy had shown no inclination to be any kind of a guard dog, but she was big and passably ugly and first impressions of her were often intimidating. She now cheerfully accepted the invitation for a walk, and they set off up the track that led to the pump house and formed the boundary between

Serge's and the LePage sugar bushes. Without a snowmobile or ATV, the hike up was surprisingly steep and long. It took a full fifteen minutes for them to reach the bend in the road that preceded the level straight-away that had been Jean-Yves undoing. Thirty yards or so up the track she found the place she was looking for. It looked much the same as she remembered it: a broken tree and a deadly cable. She had not been back since that dreadful morning, and then, the game warden had been the designated adjudicator of the scene and she and Gilles had been able to avoid examining it.

She stood staring at the tree and the cable. With no snow pack left to support the broken tree, it now lay half into the road, the lethal wire harmlessly draped along the ground. Just beyond, the scars and debris created by the impact of the crash were proof of the snowmobile's speed. Simone imagined the shock that Jean-Yves would have felt as the cable, caught under his helmet, yanked him off his snowmobile and snapped his neck in one terrifying moment.

She forced herself to concentrate on what she was looking at.

She knew this cable well. She had helped Serge install it when he expanded his lease and built the new pump house. It was a line-tensioning tie-back, carefully positioned to keep the sap lines in place and taut, and as with any of Serge's cables that crossed a traveled track, it had been strung high enough to avoid any danger to riders, crossing the track at a spot where the trail dipped slightly and a safe height was easily established.

Her attention was taken momentarily by Ivy, who was grunting and snuffling at the edge of the track. Simone knew that porcupines were a constant presence in these woods, and had no faith in Ivy's ability to resist the impulse to pounce on anything moving. She was snapping a precautionary leash on her collar when something caught her eye. Under the leaves that Ivy had been exploring was a shard of pink surveyor's tape. As she picked it up, a clear memory came back. Serge was a belts-and-suspenders kind of guy, and in addition to stringing his tie-back wires at a safe height, he always took the added precaution of hanging long ribbons of colored tape from the wires wherever they crossed a trail—visible backup warnings of the cable's presence.

She looked down at the cable. The scrap of ribbon that she held was all that there was—the long warning ribbons were gone. An uneasy feeling was marrying up to Mattie's whispered pronouncement that she would see, and understand, that all was not right. She thought back again to the day when she and Serge had installed this cable. The need for it had been clear. The main line, carrying fresh sap from the pump house to the camp, was twist-tied to a supporting heavy-duty cable. To prevent sap from collecting in low spots, the cable was strung with a carefully planned steady drop, secured to trees or posts where trees were not available. Where the cable and the line it supported turned corners, a tie-back was needed to keep the line taut. Since Serge's new line ran along the edge of the woods road, the tie-back had, by necessity, been strung across the track. She had been responsible for adding the streamers of tape, now nowhere to be seen.

She remembered Serge finding a yellow birch with twin trunks. He had secured the wire around the nearest one, using old, wide truck tie-down straps to minimize damage to the tree. As backup, mindful of the havoc that moose and wind could wreak, he had then added a second strap, anchoring the first trunk to the one behind it. For the cable to be at the lethal height that had caught Jean-Yves, this connection would have to have failed somehow, as the broken trunk should have been held up by the second one. The game warden's report had been certain that the accident was the result of the anchor tree coming down, but now that Simone recalled the details of the installation, she could not see how the damn cable had got to where it was. Why had the broken trunk not been held up as Serge had intended?

She moved toward the trees themselves, aware that she was now looking for evidence of something sinister and frightening. Rather than tie Ivy to a sapling to prevent her from harassing wildlife, she kept hold of the leash, glad of her solid presence. Following the broken trunk from the point where the cable was still attached, she could find no evidence of the strap that had anchored it to its sister. It was just plain missing, like the pink tape. With increasing dread, she moved her examination of the tree to the break, close to the ground, that had brought it down. At first glance, the break appeared uneven and ragged, like any other wind-induced fail, but as she looked closer she was aware that the splintered edges accounted for only part of the break. Low to the ground, and disguised by mud and leaves, were a series of sharp-edged cuts that could only have been made by an axe—wielded by a person intent on bringing down the tree.

Fucking hell, she thought to herself, some bastard engineered this and tried to make it look natural. She checked the second trunk for any sign of the support strap that should have been there. Nothing. She thought back to the day of the accident, which she now was realizing had likely been no accident at all. Fresh snow had fallen the night before, covering evidence of tampering. Above the snow, the break looked natural, and in the midst of the chaos of the moment, no one had noticed the missing strap and ribbon.

Simone's knees had temporarily lost their ability to hold her up, and she found herself sitting on the fallen tree with Ivy's anxious face in her own. She pulled the dog toward her.

They fucking killed him, was all she could think.

She sat until she felt strength returning to her legs, her mind racing with the thought that she could be looking at evidence of murder. Mattie was right. This had been a deliberate act, and she and the speechless boy were the only ones who knew. His faith in her made her blood run faster and put her mind back to work.

Those murderous bastards had waited for a snowy night to cover their tracks before they tampered with the tree, knowing that Jean-Yves would come flying around that corner and not see the wire without its warning ribbons. But why? What had the boys seen that had put them in this danger? Was fear for his own life part of the reason that Mattie had reacted so badly? What was she supposed to do next?

She pulled herself to her feet and took another long look at the scene, but found nothing new. The tree had been detached from its support and partially chopped through, then pulled until it broke, bringing the cable to head-height of a snowmobiler. They had cut off the pink tape, carelessly dropping one piece into the snow. All they had to do then was to wait. Simone dug her phone out of her pocket and photographed the cut base of the tree, recognizing that while this was damning evidence, it was no proof of a crime. There has to be more, she figured. She had to find whatever it was that the boys saw, or she had nothing more than a broken tree to suggest foul play by the LePages.

She listened for a moment. Nobody around. Emboldened by rising anger and the opportunity presented by the emptiness of the woods, she set off down the track toward the camps. Keeping Ivy close by her, she cut into the trees before she reached the Thibodeau camp, bushwhacking down the slope, threading her way through maple saplings and hobblebush until she stumbled into the LePages' back yard. She paused to check once again that she was alone. Still no sign of anyone. Hadn't Steve said that no one had been in for weeks? She took a look around. A collection of run-down buildings and clutter confronted her. Main sap lines ran in familiar fashion from the trees above them into the main building. There was an old woodshed, a pile of dented, discarded syrup barrels, a padlocked machine shed, and a caved-in galvanized storage tank. Making her way cautiously around the old barrels, she arrived at the front of the camp, negotiating another pile of rusting gear and abandoned truck parts. The door to the camp was also conspicuously padlocked. Deciding to see what else she could learn, Simone stepped up to the nearest window and peered into the dim interior of the camp. Cobwebs, the side view of the boiler, assorted bits of old furniture, and a dismantled pressure filter were visible. Nothing interesting there, she thought. Battered but useable equipment. She had seen good syrup made in similar situations. The windows to the living quarters had blinds drawn over them and yielded no information. She asked herself what she had hoped to find. Piles of packaged drugs stacked for her to photograph? Unlikely, she realized. If these morons were using the camp as cover for a drug-moving operation and the boys had spotted something dodgy, she was probably not going to find anything convincing by peering through windows.

Behind her, someone sneezed, making her heart jump out of her chest. Hoping to look nonchalant, she stepped away from the window and turned to see who had discovered her trespassing. The portly form of a large porcupine, disturbed by their presence and heading out of harm's way toward the woodshed, was all that she saw. Jeeesus, she thought, waiting for her heartbeat to return to normal. I need to get out of here.

She thanked her stars that she still had Ivy on a leash. This was not the day to deal with a dog with a muzzle full of quills. Reassured that the porcupine was her only observer, she took another look around the yard. That the camp had been in operation was evident from the cluster of barrels waiting for collection on the one reasonably level space outside the garage doors into the working part of the camp. Simone's inner inspector was on autopilot as she ran her eyes over the stash. They appeared to have been randomly assembled, unlike Serge's, which were lined up in neat sequential order, satisfying his own sense of tidiness and facilitating easy counting by inspectors and buyers alike. Not that it really mattered. They would be logged onto a pickup sheet by Braisethwaites in any case, the driver painstakingly noting every barrel number in the order loaded. Any question about quantity of barrels collected could be easily checked against this record. From sheer force of habit, Simone paused to see how well these barrels were labeled. Her expert eye found #113 near the front of the stack, dated just a couple of days after Serge and Gilles had called it quits on the season. She noted with some amusement that the first ten barrels were lined up in numerical order at the back of the stack. From there, the rest were in higgledy-piggledy groups and crooked lines. Looks like they started out with good intentions, she thought, and lost it as the season got busier. Still, nothing out of the ordinary there. Syrup could be certified organic as long as its production process followed the rules. Tidiness was not one of them, provided standards of cleanliness could be met.

Checking once again that she was unobserved, she strode quickly down the camp drive to the road. From there it was a short walk to Serge's camp and the safety of her truck. She loaded Ivy onto her seat, locked up the camp, returned the key to its brick, and turned the truck toward the Golden Road.

She contemplated finding Steve and telling him what she had discovered, but could think of no way he could help beyond alerting authorities, and she was aware that she had no proof that the LePage boys were responsible for the damage to the tree. Where the hell is Serge when I need him? she asked herself. He would certainly understand the significance of Mattie's claim. I need to talk to him, she thought, but he is in freaking New Hampshire and I have to be back at the greenhouse in the morning. Nothing for it but to hit the road and work something out as I drive, she decided.

5

Simone's hope for a thoughtful drive down an empty road turned out to be unrealistic from the outset. A mile after leaving her uncle's camp, her head full of crazy conspiracy theories and unsettling realities, she was distracted by a convoy of huge logging trucks heading for the Canadian border with loads of winter-cut logs. Her irritation at being driven into the muddy edges of the roads by cowboy truckers who knew damn well that they actually did own the road—or at least the companies they were contracted to did—grew into hot rage when she recognized the loads they were carrying. Far from being the customary spruce and fir sticks, destined for Canadian lumber mills, the trucks were stacked with mature maple logs. Simone had heard complaints from syrup producers, whose tap leases were being jacked up at a rate that was threatening their survival, that the hot-money jerks from away who now owned the land and pulled all the strings wanted quicker returns on their investments. If they could push the lease holders out of business they could clear-cut good maple stands for fast profit. Bloodsucking bastards, thought Simone. They don't know shit about the value of these woods. This is prime maple forest up here. Cut it down and you've destroyed a way of life, an ecosystem, and a source of the finest natural sweetener in the world—not to mention a giant sustainable source of revenue for the state and the carbon sequestration that goes with it. I bet those hedge-fund assholes are paying through the nose for organic syrup at their fancy city health food stores too. Ignorant tools. They should get out of their Beemers and Lexuses and spend a winter up here and see how hard these people work to make that syrup, and how beautiful these maple forests are.

Distracted by her fury at this perceived disrespect for the woods and the people who work in them, she pulled herself back to the question of what the hell was going on at the LePage setup. They were an anomaly among the Canadians who made up the vast majority of syrup producers in this part of Maine. What explained the dilapidation that was so evident there? Perhaps it was the fact that their sugar bush was a mediocre stand of trees, low on the slope and stressed by poorly draining soil. Or maybe the fact that these trees had been tapped for many years—the two goons running the place now were the third generation on that lease, and long-term tapping led to some inevitable decline in productivity. Either way it did not appear to be a thriving enterprise. And now they were up to something dangerous and scary.

She tried to make sense of the idea that the camp was somehow being used by the suspected drug-selling uncles, but it did not go well. The notion that anyone could use this remote and tightly watched place for something so obviously nefarious was absurd. The only topic of conversation she had ever heard around the camps, apart from the arcana of syrup making, was what the other producers were doing. Nothing happened that was not instantly broadcast over the local grapevine. The border guards had to deal with only a handful of people crossing in and out per day, and they pretty much knew everything that the regulars were up to, including the flavor of the pie that some family member had brought in to feed the weary workers. And the very idea that these two incompetent idiots who could barely run a maple camp could be trusted with concealing an illegal activity did not ring true. She was unable to conquer the feeling that she was in over her head here. She needed to share her discovery of the felled tree and tampered-with cable with Serge, who she hoped would know what the next move should be. She returned to musing about the overall crappiness of the LePage enterprise. It offended her that anyone should let a camp degenerate into such a slovenly state. Her DNA, shared with Serge and Mattie, commanded her to keep everything orderly and spit-shined.

As she contemplated what she had seen at the LePage camp, something at the very back of her mind was nagging at her, demanding attention. Putting all speculation about drug lords and opiates aside, she ran the internal video of her brief exploration of the camp. Sap lines, boiler, filters, generator shed: nothing out of the ordinary there. It was when the picture of the cluster of sap barrels came up she realized what was bothering her. The last barrel she had seen was labeled number 113, and in that disorganized stash there could well have been even more, and that was a problem. To her knowledge, Serge had made only 120 or so barrels, and he had better trees and a lot more of them. Even allowing for the somewhat premature termination of his season, he should have made a hell of a lot more syrup than the LePage boys. She turned her mind's eye to the barrel stack at LePages again, trying to find a simple explanation in their numbering system. Maybe they had skipped a bunch of numbers, or had some esoteric counting method, but strict sequential numbering was the standard rule, and her quick scan had not noted anything unusual. Weird. Okay, maybe they got lucky somehow, but it made no sense, and the inspector in her did not like it. At least this was familiar ground for her, and her mind ran on through the inspection verification rituals. The last part of any inspection was the audits. Producers were required to maintain a log of each barrel's "date of birth," as she liked to explain to reluctant operators. Each barrel gets a dated label with its sequential number, which can be traced back to the daily production log. Additionally, sales records—typically the barrel-by-barrel pickup record made by the buyer's driver—must be reconciled with the production log. She was used to anxious producers sweating over their incomplete records, unable to explain small discrepancies between production and sales counts. The usual sheepish explanation for a missing barrel or two was that they bottled or canned them up "for family." This resulted in admonishments to record the barrel numbers so used, and a reassurance that sneaking syrup into Canada for Christmas gifts was not the concern of the organic inspector, provided they could account for the disposition of every barrel. To find that one or two barrels had gone missing was not a cause for huge concern. It was the possibility of finding too many barrels that was now raising red flags in Simone's mind.

It was one thing to wonder whether these boys had squeezed unlikely amounts of sap out of their sugar bush and another to figure out how they could do it. Tapping a whole lot of undersized trees was a possibility, but inspections included a check of tapping practices and wholesale violations would, she hoped, be easily caught. Besides, the land management companies did their own checks of taps and generally required the same standards to be met. Hiding enough nonregulation trees to make a substantial difference would not be easy, but maybe these two were dumb enough to try it. She stayed on the subject for the next hour, running over all the options she could think of to explain her suspicion of the LePages' over-production. There was really no easy answer. Don't jump to conclusions, she warned herself. Review what you know in an orderly manner. More information was what she needed.

Simone had formulated a plan by the time she reached paved road at the foot of Baxter State Park, the protected rectangle of land encompassing Mount Katahdin, Maine's iconic peak that marks the northern limit of the Appalachian Trail. Curiosity alone was enough to drive her to seek explanations for her questions, and on this matter she was on home turf. She herself had never inspected the LePages, but other good inspectors had been there, and years of inspection reports would be on file at MOMP. As an inspector, she would have access to prior reports, and she could, at the very least, look at tap counts and production totals for the past years and see what they told her.

She would pay a visit to the MOMP office, but it would have to wait for the upcoming greenhouse weekend to be done. She could maybe beg a bed off Linda in Skowhegan, home of the MOMP headquarters, and catch up on work news and gossip. She debated how she would explain her need to rummage through files, but left that problem for another day. She would find a way and hope to discover something useful.

She thought of Mattie, distressed and maybe frightened, trusting her to help him. Paralleling her desire to find out what he had seen and what had caused Jean-Yves's death was an understanding that prematurely opening up a can of worms of accusations would rain hell on Mattie. She needed to have a stronger case—more evidence of foul play, conclusions, even—so he could be spared the pain of interrogation. That was why he had found the courage to tell her what little he had. He knew she wouldn't start wild rumors that could bring inquisitors who might try to force him to talk. Come to think of it, she didn't want to be made to justify her suspicions yet, either. She would wait to track Serge down until she had more to go on, and then together they could work out what to do.

That thought notwithstanding, she felt the need to keep Mattie in the loop. With good phone reception established, she pulled into the parking lot of the Baxter General Store to drop him a text: *I'm on it. Hang in there and don't worry. Ivy is on the job too and sends love.*

Ivy, however, seemed to have snacks on her mind. A whiff of burgers and hot dogs was reaching her through the truck's open window.

"I'll split a cheeseburger with you, Piggy," Simone conceded.

There was time to dally a little at the edge of Millinocket Lake and check for loons. It was probably still too early to find parents with chicks, a sight that never grew old for Simone, but with luck and the help of binoculars she might spot this year's returning birds. As they shared the burger, she scanned the surface of the lake but found nothing more interesting than a pair of mallards and the tips of old logs that stuck up out of the water, remnants of the days when logs were driven down the rivers and boomed across the lakes. Those road-hog truck drivers owed their living to the environmental effort that had banned river drives. I guess a bunch of new roads is better than polluted rivers and beat-up river banks, Simone reflected. And besides, most of the truckers weren't road hogs anyway, she knew. She had to give up the unrealistic wish that the woods could be left untouched. That ship had sailed a long time ago.

With the rest stop over and the day closing in, she loaded the obliging dog back into the truck and headed for the town of Millinocket and on to Highway 95. LaGrange was an easy fifty miles of highway from here, and she needed to get back to work.

"You are expensive and useless," she told Ivy. "Good thing you are pretty."

She had to thank Steve for that thought. It pleased her to know that they both found the gaping alligator look-alike appealing. She would maybe get a good photo of the big grin and send it to him.

* * *

It was a full five days before Simone could get away from the greenhouse. By promising to come back later and help put the operation to bed for the rest of the year, she had been given the all-clear to leave. Glad to be free of the demands of the business, she put aside, for now, the recurring question of how she would support herself for the rest of the year, a problem given some greater urgency by Ivy's presence. Feeding the beast was not free. She would use a visit to MOMP to get recommendations from Linda that could be leveraged into some starter-level farm inspections in the ever-growing world of small organic farms in Maine.

This resurgence of family farming was even breathing new life into the forlorn small towns she passed through en route to Skowhegan. This is the forgotten, dead center of Maine, possessing neither vacation-worthy ski mountains and lakeside resorts nor the obvious tourist attractions of rocky coastline and lobster pounds. It is the home of shuttered mills and defunct chicken barns, its former agricultural prosperity surrendered decades ago to the corporate enterprises of the Midwest and beyond. But new signs, announcing farmers' markets and pick-your-own fruit opportunities, hinted at hopeful possibilities for the future. About damn time, Simone thought, for people to realize that food grown right here was a far better bet than trucked-in big ag products from California and beyond. If there is one thing we should be able to do up here, she thought, not for the first time, it's feed ourselves. On that note, she stopped at the Gifford's Ice Cream stand in Skowhegan for a tub of maple-walnut as an offering to Linda, from whom she had secured the promise of a sofa and a sleeping bag for as long as she wanted it—provided this new dog she had heard about did not beat up on the two house cats.

Linda was at work when they reached the MOMP office. With maple inspections now complete, she was busy with the follow-up demands of the certification process, sending out letters to each operator with the appropriate assessment of their compliance with organic standards.

"Good grief, what have you got there?" was her greeting. Simone was about to say "maple walnut" when she realized that Linda was giving Ivy a long, doubtful look. Ivy was cruising the small kitchen area, making loud snorting noises as she shoved her broad snout into corners, hoping to find anything spilled and forgotten.

"Ivy. Say hi to Linda, and be nice—she's our boss and we need work," Simone commanded, and the obliging dog waddled over to Linda's desk, wagging her entire rear end and smiling toothily.

"You couldn't find anything better looking?" Linda asked, as Ivy pressed one whole side of herself against her, providing maximum surface area for convenient petting. Linda rubbed her flank and she grunted and wriggled, prompting more vigorous efforts by Linda. The feedback loop having been successfully established, Ivy flopped onto her back and offered her wide pink belly to complete the process.

"Watch out, attack dog," warned Simone. "They ban brutes like her in some countries, so beware."

"I would ban anything that farts like that," Linda commented, trying to push the recumbent dog away from her.

"Sorry. I should stop sharing burgers with her—huge mistake," Simone apologized. She snapped her fingers at Ivy, awakening a memory of earlier lessons, and the dog, sensing displeasure, struggled to her feet to sit solemnly by Simone, the model of obedient repentance.

"Good beast." Simone rubbed her ears. "Now stay out of trouble while I bother Linda."

She had delivered a somewhat garbled explanation for her visit over the phone, telling Linda that with the loss of Jean-Yves and—for now, anyway, Mattie—as helpers, Serge was looking for advice on streamlining his operation and wanted her input. Simone had asked if she could read through prior reports to get the inspectors' views of his business and its recent history. Linda had no problems with this. As an inspector, all information on file was covered by Simone's confidentiality agreement, and as an authorized representative on Serge's Organic System Plan she would be entitled to see anything in his file.

"Knock yourself out," was Linda's offer. "You know where the files are. Just leave it all as you find it, and put that ice cream in the freezer before you do anything else. I've only got veggies for us later and that will help boost the calorie count."

For the next hour Simone dutifully read through several years' worth of inspection reports and Organic System Plan updates in the Thibodeau file, finding nothing she did not already know and wondering what excuse she could use to take the LePage file out. She was leery of being seen crossing lines that kept inspectors from becoming judges. It was way beyond her job to be examining files for irregularities in the operation, and she knew that Linda would question such a request.

Still, reading through Serge's file was a good exercise. She duly noted the neatly drawn map lines—odd multi-fingered depictions of the location and tap counts of each line. Serge had two major sections of sugar bush: the older trees that had initially been tapped by his father and the newer trees higher on the ridge. The lines from the old section ran directly into the camp, but the newer ones fed into the pump station at the end of the fateful road, the sap from there being pumped through a main line to the camp. The annual reports recorded minor fluctuations in tap counts as Serge removed taps from sick or broken trees and added a few new ones as undersized trees graduated to the required diameter, painstakingly checking the count every year by the number of spouts used. The old stand averaged around ten thousand taps and the new one closer to twelve thousand.

The statistic that Simone was looking for, always present in the audit section of the reports, was the pounds of syrup yielded every year per tap. This, she knew, was the measure of the health of the trees and the efficiency of the operation. In a good season, with robust trees and leakproof taps and lines, a sugar bush up in these woods could yield over seven pounds per tap. One boastful producer had claimed to Simone that he could get ten pounds if he was allowed to tap only the best trees, but the land manager required him to tap all trees that made the size grade, as their take from his business was based on tap count, not tap yield. Simone doubted that he was right, but it was true that pulling taps from unproductive trees did not make producers popular with their lessors.

Back when Serge had only the older trees, his yields had been in the respectable, average range of three-and-a-half to four pounds per tap. His big upgrade came with the addition of the new trees. Simone had helped him install the new lines and upgrade the old ones, gradually replacing the "drops"—the short tubes that carry sap from the spout to the connector lines—and simultaneously changing over to single-use spouts. Using new spouts every year was a cost that Serge was reluctant to embrace, but the reduction in leaks at the tap site immediately translated into better yields, and besides, it gave him an easy way to derive an accurate tap count, as he filled his pockets with empty hundred-spout bags.

Checking the records since the new installations had been completed, Simone found yields had risen respectably. The previous year, the last for which yield totals were available, he had made 5.8 pounds per tap. Granted, it had been a banner year. Simone had collected high yield numbers at all the producers she had inspected, but Serge had been pleased to see that his investments were paying off. That was last year, when Mattie and Jean-Yves had been full-time crew, checking leaks and keeping equipment running smoothly. She felt her heart miss several beats as she saw again the dead boy on the trail and realized what a mass of misery and lost hopes they were all still facing.

Linda was making get-ready-to-leave noises and Ivy had stirred from her position at Simone's feet. She was glad to be distracted from the recognition of what lay behind her mission here. Linda's veggies, a bottle of wine, and all the ice cream they could eat were better things to contemplate, and she put the Thibodeau file back together and stashed it in the cabinet, eying the name tabs on the other files as she did. LePage was right there. I'll get back to you, she promised it as she closed the drawer.

Back at Linda's house, Simone clipped the leash to Ivy's collar and took the usual precautionary turn around her thick neck.

"If you so much as look cross-eyed at Linda's cats, I will take your ugly face off and feed it to the crows," Simone warned Ivy, whose delighted response suggested that Simone had not hit the right note in her admonition.

"Just behave like a civilized dog, okay?" she pleaded.

Her doubts about Ivy's ability to distinguish between pet cats and squirrels turned out to be unfounded. The two cats, rugged Maine coons, were unimpressed by Ivy's enthusiastic entrance. Having retreated to high ground to assess the situation, it was soon clear to them that this was no challenge. Too bad that cats can tell that she is a harmless pushover, thought Simone, while most humans jump to the stupid prejudgment that she is pure fighting killer and should not be allowed to live.

Supper and wine consumed, and promises of references and help with future jobs secured from Linda, she and Ivy found room together on the pull-out sofa bed. Simone had the sense that, given time to delve into the LePage records, she would learn enough to at least put some clarity into her muddled thinking. She mumbled something to Linda about wanting to make more notes and fell asleep against the comforting mass of her dog.

* * *

As it turned out, elaborate excuses for reading the LePage file weren't needed. The next morning, Linda handed Simone the office phone, told her to take messages and to apologize to anyone who stopped by looking for her, and took off to make an overdue visit to a nearby maple candy maker who was looking to certify her sweets as organic.

Okay, here goes, Simone thought. This is where I find out if I am imagining things or if there really is something fishy going on. She pulled out the LePage file and, to her dismay, found her pulse was racing. What the fuck, she told herself, you are reading inspection reports, not facing down El Chapo.

"Hey, Fat Face." She called Ivy from her exploration of the kitchen. "Come do your job. Keep the bad guys away."

Ivy ambled over, needing no further bidding, and settled herself comfortably on Simone's feet. Simone got to work. She figured she had a couple of hours before she would have to explain herself further.

The papers in the file were stacked in familiar order. Robert's recent report, filed a couple of days after he had inspected the two camps, was on the top. Attached to it was a copy of the subsequent findings letter from Linda to the producer—her notice to them of problems or omissions arising from their inspection. Putting that aside for now, Simone turned to the Inspector Questions document beneath the report. This, the essential pre-inspection heads-up note from MOMP to the inspector, highlighted issues, usually arising from the past year's inspection, that MOMP identified as important and in need of attention at the next inspection. The communication loop thus guaranteed, if everything worked right, some continuity between years and from one inspector to the next. This was where Simone liked to start when preparing for an inspection. She reckoned that if she did nothing else right, checking on whatever it was that HQ deemed of interest was a priority. Since the majority of the maple producers had the inspection process pretty much nailed down, these questions, if any, were typically minor, like a request to follow up on a missing receipt for new equipment or an overlooked cleaning log. When Simone found the Inspector Questions that Robert would have read in his preparation, she found a note from Linda followed by two demands, with bullet points and bolded headings:

Please check on the following (see also letter from last year):
1. **Have maps been updated?**
2. **Can tap counts be verified?**

Hmm, thought Simone. Taps and maps—not usually a problem with established producers since these represent such basic data. And Linda sounded serious here. Let's see what Robert found, she decided.

A quick scan of the checklist part of Robert's report revealed a number of "see narrative" notes against the boxes where the presence of correct information on maps, taps, and other basics were normally checked. She flipped to the end of the checklist to the narrative section, where inspectors can comment on exceptional circumstances or provide background for problems they encounter. Robert had had a lot to say:

Inspection scheduled near end of season. No sap running but camp was in operation boiling sap previously collected. Only one of the LePage brothers (Bernard) present so unable to accompany inspector on tree inspection. Saw trees around camp and along Line B.

NOTE: During subsequent tour of sugar bush and remote pump station of abutting operation (with Serge Thibodeau), top of LePage sugar bush was seen and far end of Line B trees inspected. Nothing of note found although lines are old. Some tapped trees marginal size (30" and 29"dbh measured). Discussion of findings not included in Exit Interview with LePage.

Well that was all interesting for a start, Simone thought. When she had left, Serge was out of sap to boil. Could be lots of reasons the LePages were boiling stored syrup, but she stuck a mental pin in that thought and moved on. What was the follow-up to Linda's questions?

In the Response to Inspector Questions box, Robert had dutifully written out his findings. (Simone liked Robert's matching use of the Bold option—creative formatting opportunities exist even in dry inspector reports.)

1. **Have maps been updated?** *Maps same as last year. Hard to decipher and appear to be out of date.*
2. **Can tap counts be verified?** *Tapping logs not complete. Bernard reported some "normal" work on lines but no significant change in tap numbers.*

So, Simone concluded, this map and tap count problem was an old one that wasn't getting resolved. She read on.

Below his basic response, Robert had added:

Letter from last year reviewed. Efforts to convey importance of verifiable records of tap counts and line locations hampered by language difficulties. Bernard LePage speaks very little English and his brother was not at the camp at time of inspection.

Well, that is just bullshit, Simone thought. Both those clowns speak decent English, having spent most of their lives trying to emulate Hollywood gangsters. And where the hell was Idiot Number 2? If they were processing sap, he couldn't have been far. But never mind that for now. There was more paperwork to read while she had the office to herself. The lack of good information on what lines went where and how many taps they served was beginning to look like more than mere sloppiness on the part of the LePages, and her interest was definitely piqued.

Next thing to check was Robert's exit interview. A duplicate form is provided to every inspector, a copy being left with the client and one going back to MOMP. Robert's tidy handwriting on the file copy confirmed the obvious. Citing the appropriate part of the National Organic

Program rule, he had observed, again, the lack of reliable map and tap count records.

So their production baseline data was crap. To trace the history, she turned back to the findings letter from the year before, and to the inspector report from that year. Well, hello, she thought, seeing Julian's name on the report. How had he made out, she wondered? She did not recognize the other name on the document, but it was standard procedure for these inspections to be done by a two-person team, and she assumed that the second name belonged to a French-speaking support person. So what had they found a year ago?

In the checklist boxes, Julian had also found problems that needed more space than a simple check would use. In the comments section on maps he had noted:

Map of sugar bush blurry and hard to decipher and tap totals possibly inaccurate as tapping log also hard to read.

That was the way to do it, she recognized. She had often found shitty records and duly reported them. She glanced at the exit interview. Julian had written:

1. ***Map of sugar bush not accurate representation of lines.***
2. ***Tap count could not be verified from records.***

Good job, Simone grudgingly admitted, reluctant to revise her opinion of him. He had reported clearly on problems and avoided the inspector's ever-present temptation to judge and prescribe. Linda's letter that had accompanied the report back to the LePages one year earlier had been clear. Following her usual greetings and thanks for their cooperation, she had stated her findings;

Conditions for Continued Certification:
Your attention is drawn to the following points of concern. Your inspector will be looking for improvements on these matters at your next inspection:

1. Please provide accurate depictions of the locations of your lines.
2. Please provide accurate tapping records.

So, obviously, this has been going on for a while, Simone concluded. Wondering how Linda had reacted to their ongoing failure to provide better records, she turned back to the newest papers in the file and retrieved the findings letter that Linda had written just weeks ago. Sure enough, the message had evolved from polite requests to a formal "Notice of Non-Compliance." As long as mere incompetence could explain poor records and the issues in question did not indicate blatant violations of organic requirements—such as exposure to contaminants that could result in a demand to immediately withdraw a product from the organic stream—it was usual for producers to be nudged and encouraged toward full compliance. This sterner step was intended to do that.

Citing the Records section of the organic rule, she gave the LePages thirty days to provide a response to her demand for verifiable records and spelled out the continuing problem of inadequate maps and tap counts. Failure to comply with her request would result in the issuance of a proposed suspension of their organic certification, her letter concluded.

Way to go, Linda, Simone thought. It occurred to her that she had never seen the question of maps and taps data produce such a tough response. It was not like Linda to climb all over a producer over sloppy maps. Just how bad were these maps? she wondered. Digging through the file she found a dog-eared and undated hand-drawn map that had obviously been there for some years. With a small guilty twinge—she was, after all, about to remove data from a file—she got out her phone and snapped a picture of it. Might be nice to study this sucker later, she thought, and I can always delete it when I am done.

She glanced at her watch and realized she'd been side-tracked. That these bozos couldn't—or wouldn't—draw a map or count spouts was no surprise, but the picture in her mind of the stack of barrels in the LePage yard brought her back to what she was really looking for. Reluctantly, as numbers and mathematics had never been her strong subjects, she went looking for the production data that might shed light on her sense that something more important was askew.

Each year, an inspector notes the quantity of syrup made to date and the tap count for the current year, but since inspections are typically carried out mid-season, and data for that year is therefore incomplete, calculations of yield per tap are necessarily based on the previous year's records. Simone searched through the papers now distributed over the whole desk until she found Robert's report again.

The yield calculations boxes that she found looked like this:

Previous year yield data:
Total tap count: 14,500 *(approx. only—see last year's report, etc.)*
Total barrels/pounds produced: 70 barrels/42,350 lbs
Verification seen? Pick-up log seen—all went to Sugar Shack—receipt not on hand
Yield #/tap: 2.92# approx

The nitpicker in Simone had her bringing up the calculator on her phone.. In the absence of a final receipt from the Sugar Shack, Robert would have calculated an approximate total by multiplying the number of barrels by 605—the estimated weight of syrup in each 55 gallon barrel, using the standard 11 pounds per gallon for syrup. Sure enough, 70 barrels times 605 pounds came out to 42,350 pounds of syrup sold by the LePages a year ago. And, to be sure, if they had 14,500 taps, their yield for that year had indeed been under 3 pounds per tap.

Less than three pounds per tap is a lousy yield, Simone told herself. Last year had been a good one, and even the poor operations had managed more than that. She checked the notes she had made the day before. Yup—Serge had managed 5.8 pounds. Three pounds, she knew, represented not much more than a break-even income. Using $2 per pound as a rough number for the price of syrup, the LePages had brought in around $84,700 last year. Subtract from that the cost of fuel, the per-tap lease (which on the Golden Road was now over a dollar), and unavoidable maintenance that even they would have to do, they were working for bare minimum wage. Even Serge would admit that if it wasn't for the low-cost labor he got from the boys (there was that awful thump in her chest again), he would have trouble justifying the time and money he spent making syrup.

So, what was the story for this year? she wondered. Granted, numbers would be a bit hazy as the season was not over when Robert inspected, but Serge had been all done and the LePage boys must have been almost done, so whatever Robert had found would provide a reasonable picture of this year's production. She went back to the pile of paperwork to see what useful information was still to be had.

In the body of the newest LePage report she found, once again with a note indicating that the count was approximate, that Robert had recorded 14,600 taps this year, with an added comment that Bernard LePage had reported the addition of "some" new trees—presumably by using trees that had achieved legal diameter for tapping. In the Barrels/Pounds Produced to Date box, he had noted *113 barrels (still processing sap)*.

Jesus, Simone thought. That was a shit ton more than they made last year, and judging by Robert's note they may have made even more than that. She briefly reviewed the numbers, with questions swirling in her head. She needed to get the meat of her discoveries into some form that she could study later.

Pulling the yellow notepad she had brought with her out from under all the LePage documents, she sketched the following chart:

LePage	This year			Last year		
	Taps	Barrels	Pounds	Taps	Barrels	Pounds
	14,600	115(?)	69,757	14,500	70	42,350

The 115 barrels for the current year was a guess, but she knew they had sap to process when Robert had been there, so she gave them two more barrels than he had counted.

With her calculator to do the work, she divided taps into pounds for this year and came up with 4.77 pounds of sap per tap. Shit and re-shit— that was a big increase over last year's crappy sub-3 pounds.

She needed a point of reference before she could digest all this information, and went back to the file cabinet for Serge's file. Following the same procedures, she added numbers for Serge to her chart.

Serge	This year			Last year		
	Taps	Barrels	Pounds	Taps	Barrels	Pounds
	22,874	184	111,504	22,901	218	132,825
Yeilds	4.87#/tap			5.8#/tap		

So the LePages had increased their yield, if these numbers were to be trusted (and she already had some trouble with that idea), while Serge's had gone down. How the hell do you figure that? she asked herself. Granted, Serge had cut his season short by a day or so, but still....

There was not time to answer her questions. As she started to put the files back in order, Linda came through the door, knocking mud off her boots on the lintel before she stepped into the office.

"Ugh," was her first utterance. "I think I ate too much maple candy. That stuff is way too sweet, but they kept feeding me samples." She looked over at Simone and Ivy, who was getting her feet under her to greet her new friend, and gestured at the scattered papers.

"Find what you needed?" she asked, taking a closer look at Simone's project.

Caught with the LePage file in full view, and encouraged by Linda's apparently unruffled response, Simone offered an explanation.

"My uncle's neighbors," she said. "You had asked if they were operating. I don't really know how they get by—they are a pain in Serge's ass anyway. I was wondering what Robert had found. It was all so bad..." She trailed off, not wanting to involve Linda in either the dreadful event of Jean-Yves's death or, until she'd had time to digest what she had found out, the questions surrounding the LePages' extraordinarily boosted yields. But she found that Linda was already ahead of her on that. Picking up Robert's report, she waved it around as if by energizing the paperwork she could get it to tell her its secrets.

"You know," she said, "Robert sent me a note after he did this inspection. It's buried in my computer, but you might be interested."

God bless Linda, Simone thought. She watched as her boss clicked around on her laptop and eventually turned it around so Simone could read the note on the screen.

Confidential to Linda from Robert Casswell, it read, followed by the date of his report. Such notes, sent to Linda with information or comments that would be kept out of the file and thus not seen by the client, were not unusual, Simone knew. She had used one herself when needing to report the creepy guy who had tried to come on to her. She concentrated on reading the text of Robert's message.

Hi Linda. A word regarding the LePage maple camp and my inspection of it. As you know, there had been a fatal snowmobile accident days before at the abutting (Thibodeau) camp. I did not know how much the LePage guys had been affected by this and found it hard to press matters. As mentioned in my report, only one brother was present. He was busy and did not appear to speak much English. I was somewhat short of time—I had to rearrange my schedule as there was nobody awake at Thibodeau's when I got there. Bernard LePage did not want to tour the woods with me. I got as much data as I could and reviewed the MOMP questions with him. When completing my report just now I noticed that the yield numbers at LePage seem too high. I believe I correctly recorded barrel counts from Bernard's production log and tap counts from his rather sketchy tapping records, but I am wondering now whether an explanation for the high yield number could be my fault.

My apologies—not sure how to fix this but thought I should let you know.

Poor bastard, thought Simone. She knew him to be a conscientious fellow, if a little short on experience. He had been thrown into a miserable situation, sent up on his own to finish up two leftover inspections under truly difficult circumstances. He had obviously not had a happy time that day.

"So, did he screw something up?" she asked Linda.

"He is a bit of a rookie, but he's careful and smart," was Linda's response. "And I don't really buy the hardship story he seemed to get from the LePage guy. If your dad and your uncle could handle an inspection, I can't see what excuse this dude had. They should have good, clean records available regardless of what else is going on. They've been dragging their feet on this whole records thing for years, anyway. I sent them an email asking for their pickup receipts for this year, so I can check that against Robert's numbers, but they are like all these guys—not great at communication out of season."

She paused for comment from Simone, who was wrestling with all kinds of thoughts, most of which still felt like fevered imaginings rather than useful comment. Getting no response, Linda closed her laptop.

"So they got a notice of noncompliance. I have to have accurate data from them to make sense of their numbers. And I shall follow up on their sales records. I gave them thirty days to get new maps to me, and they are about out of time on that one, so I guess I'm also planning an unannounced visit to nail some of this stuff down—get an inspector to do a complete tap count and tree check—but you know how complicated that gets."

An unannounced inspection was a routine way to check on suspected or unresolved compliance issues, but the situation with the maple camps led to difficult logistics. Even unannounced entry onto a client's property had to be made in the presence of the producer, and given that the client in this case lived, out of season, on the other side of the Canadian border, an unannounced inspection needed a whole lot of advanced planning and coordination with the client.

"Yeah. Tough one," Simone agreed.

Offering yet another comment that the LePage camp was a piece of shit and she had never liked the two boys, Simone tidied up the files and returned them to their proper place. She felt the need to explain to Linda how out of the norm the LePages were. She had spent too much time up in those woods not to recognize how much she valued and respected just about every other producer there. The French-Canadians she had grown up around were kind, hard-working, unpretentious people whose company she preferred, mostly, to their brash and mouthy American counterparts. Her efforts to convey this to Linda sounded too much like the promo for a National Geographic exploration of a little-known people, and she gave up.

"We all have our prejudices, I guess," she concluded. 'I must be more of a Canuck than I realized."

Linda, who had enough experience to recognize that jerks and honest people were evenly distributed across ethnic lines, decided not to point out that Simone's own cranky attitude somewhat belied her view of her Canadian homies. Must get it from her mother, Linda reasoned, but never mind. A certain amount of edginess was useful for survival, and she had never had reason to doubt Simone's honesty or determination.

For her part, Simone was anxious to leave. She had stashed her notes in her backpack and wanted time to sort out what she had discovered. She prodded Ivy with her toe and thanked Linda for letting her into the files.

"We gotta head out," she said. "Places to go." She hoped she was conveying the impression of a busy life, rather than the job-free prospect that she faced at that moment. Ivy cast a last hopeful glance around the kitchen and followed her to the truck.

* * *

Simone's overwhelming need was for a quiet place to sit and consider both the information she had gathered and the options facing her. She aimed for the pizza-and-whoopie pies shack on the bank of the Kennebec River on the way out of Skowhegan. A neon Open sign hung below its hand-hewn wooden name, The Lazy Loon. "For God's sake," Simone asked Ivy as they pulled into a parking spot, "can't Mainers open a business without invoking loons, moose, or lobsters?" There had been a Roadkill Café up in Greenville for a while but that had apparently gone the way of its menu. Oh, well, at least this place was quiet mid-morning. She left the truck in the shade, cracked the windows, and told Ivy there would be a treat for her if she didn't eat the seat covers.

A couple of Harley riders were putting away a huge Hawaiian pizza as she walked in, but the table in the corner was empty. To the "What can I get you, hon," greeting from the plump lady at the counter, she requested coffee and a muffin and settled herself with a view of the river and a chance to think.

Start with the facts, she told herself. The LePage boys' yield numbers were all wrong. This could be Robert's error, but her mental picture of the stack of barrels, plus Robert's known careful work habits, left her feeling that all wrong was right. There was definitely something dodgy about their line and tap records. Are they just sloppy record keepers or are they hiding something, or both? And what about the business with Tommy—the second brother—not being there and Bernard claiming he didn't speak English and couldn't go into the woods with Robert? That all added up to a heap of bull.

Other bits of information were demanding to be noticed. The LePages had reported an early sap run and, apparently, plenty of sap at the end of the season too. So how the fuck do you account for that? Granted, their trees were out of the wind and probably caught even more early-season sun than Serge's, so maybe they did get a jump on the season. Also, plausibly, the late boiling could be explained if they had just let sap sit until they had time to process it. Most producers avoided holding sap, as bacterial activity could result in a lower grade of finished syrup, but there were always circumstances that couldn't be helped, and boiling off a big run days later was not that unusual.

To give him credit, Bernard had apparently acknowledged that they'd added a token number of new taps this year, but nowhere near enough to account for the big rise in production. Even if the new trees were super-producers they couldn't add that much sap.

She knew she was avoiding drawing any conclusions. Her habit and training was simply to observe and report and to leave judgment-making to people further up the food chain. But this was not an inspection, and she was already coloring way outside the lines. As long as there was information to assemble, she could stay where she was comfortable, gathering information, so she opened the photo she had taken that morning on her phone and peered at the picture of the LePage map. Blurry and inadequate did not do it justice. It was little more than a child's scribble. There was a crude box labeled *cabane* and some wobbly depictions of sap lines that appeared to be labeled A and B. Line A ran due west, apparently along the foot of the ridge, and was attached to a spider's web of lines that extended out toward the Canadian border. Line B was shorter and carried sap from the trees that grew above the camp and up to the road—that road—that marked the boundary between the LePage and the Thibodeau leases. Both lines fed directly into the camp. There were no remote pump stations. Robert had looked at trees near the camp and then again along the road when he had been up there with Serge. Line A, which drew from more distant trees, had not been inspected beyond the camp.

So could they be tapping a whole bunch of trees that they are not reporting? You would have to be pretty damn stupid to think you could get away with that, as both the woods management company and MOMP would sooner or later catch up with you. This year they had got lucky. Their inspection had been delayed by the chaotic events, and the inspector had been a lone guy who might be easily intimidated, but tree inspections by the leasing company would be a different matter since tap counts were their bread and butter. Simone did not doubt that the LePages were dumb as a bag of hammers, but they had a certain canniness to them and she doubted they would make such an elementary mistake. She reminded herself that they had reported the addition of a few trees, which was in itself unusual. Serge's tree count typically went down slightly over the years. Losses to storm damage and poor health were likely to out-run the recruitment of new trees, as maples on these cold hills grew ridiculously slowly. Given that the LePage trees were a lot like Serge's older stand—stressed by wet soil and a long history of tapping— she found it hard to understand how they could be adding trees without adding new territory.

True, Robert had not managed a thorough tour of the woods, but such inspection as he had made had not revealed an obvious addition of tons of new trees. But, she reminded herself, they had cooked up bogus excuses for making Robert's inspection of the sugar bush difficult, so maybe they were hiding something up there.

At least, she concluded, she knew what questions she wanted answered now. She had to find out how—and, at a pinch, whether—they were getting such high yields, and then whether this had anything to do with the alarm that Mattie had sounded.

She wrapped a crumb of muffin up in its paper, paid her bill and returned the nice lady's wish that she "have a good one," and went back out to the truck. Ivy was the model of devoted guard dog—fast asleep in Simone's seat and barely stirring as she opened the door.

"Out you get, chubs," Simone commanded, rewarding an ungainly shuffle out of the truck with the muffin crumb. "You need a walk and I need some fresh air."

The two of them walked slowly down the path that ran along the river in the shade of old white pines. Sensing their approach, a merganser mother and her endless stream of offspring shot out from under the bank and took off through the fast water, paddling frantically to the calm of an eddy below an island a few yards into the river. Simone reminded Ivy that the ban on harassing small creatures extended to the feathered variety, and got an apologetic tail wag in response. "The rule that it's better to ask for forgiveness than permission doesn't apply to pit bulls," she told Ivy, "so you can sit here and behave while I call your uncle Serge." Time to report to the generals, she told herself.

She felt confident now that she had something concrete to work with, but how and why the LePages were boosting their yields was a mystery to her. Actually, the why was easily answered. The way they had been going, their business was barely viable. But how? And more to the point, what had Mattie and Jean-Yves seen? She wanted help from Serge's calm and knowledgeable mind. More than that, she wanted to dump the whole project onto someone else. She had done what she could do. She had found reason to suspect the LePages had somehow messed with the tree that had yanked Jean-Yves off his sled, and her access to inspection files had yielded valuable information. Before she could stomach any further sleuthing, she needed someone who would share the weight with her. Right now, she needed a break. She felt the pull of the comfy home in Liberty and the possibility that her mother, given adequate opportunity and incentive, could offer her real support in her quest for a more stable income—and life.

For once in his life, Serge answered his phone on the second ring.

"Hey, Uncle," Simone said. "I need to talk to you about LePages. There's something going on up there, I think, maybe." She faltered, still aware that despite the discovery of the cut tree and the unearthing of the funky yield data, she was about to sound like a conspiracy theorist. Surprisingly, instead of asking a bunch of questions, Serge was ready with a suggestion.

"Two days," he said. "Come up to camp with me. I have to be there Monday—Braisethwaites is coming in to pick up. I'm going in Sunday night. Come talk to me. I'll be glad of the company."

Two days, thought Simone. Time to get up there and maybe catch a night with Gilles in Jackman on the way.

"Okay, I'll see you there. Thanks," she said. "And I'll bring some food." Supplies would be low at the camp and Marie-Noëlle's hands too full to send food for two with Serge.

The prospect of sharing her scraps of evidence that the LePage boys were up to something and that Jean-Yves and Mattie had somehow gotten themselves involved, lifted a weight from her shoulders. She walked back up the river to the truck and held the door for Ivy, who now could make a surprisingly agile leap onto her seat.

"We spend too much time in this thing," she confided to the dog. "We need a better answer. What do you say? One more trip up to the woods and we'll find a luxury life somewhere." She looked at Ivy's insouciant grin. What does she care? she thought. She loves riding around in the truck.

She checked the time. Still plenty of day left. They could take a slow ride up to Jackman and get there for supper. A weekend with the ancestor might be a good thing. He had definitely been a good coworker at Serge's and maybe it was time to see whether her level of irritation at his brother had permanently subsided. Don't get your hopes up, she cautioned herself, knowing she would at least be able to get some more detail out of him about the end of the season and Robert's inspection.

"Here we go. Seat belts on," she told Ivy as she pulled onto the highway and turned the truck back toward Skowhegan. Reminded of her father's eating habits, she stopped at the strip mall health food store on the north end of town. In the depressed economy of central Maine, she figured that anyone brave enough to attempt to run an alternative food-source store deserved all the help they could get. She found local cheese, a dauntingly dark and dense sourdough loaf, a bunch of new carrots and some fresh greens, plus a six-pack of local beer. Mainers may be only slowly coming around to the value of good local veggies, she reflected, but the microbrew business had taken off like a rocket, and there was a brewery in every town now. Shopping for Serge would have to wait until Saint-Georges, as transporting vegetables into Canada was not allowed and she had no desire to see expensive food disappear into the border station.

With the inevitable granola bar for sustenance (one day, she told herself, I shall be living on real meals and not road snacks), she once again pointed the truck up Route 201. The adventure-seekers were out in force now, gaudy in their high-tech fabrics as they assembled canoes and gear in the riverside parking lots. The rafting company buses outnumbered logging trucks at this time of year, their owners clambering over each other to take advantage of the high water levels. Simone regarded them as harmless, but knew that there was not enough money in the world to get her into a rubber raft with a bunch of screaming strangers. It occurred to her that she should let Gilles know she was coming—and that Ivy wouldn't turn down some nice steak tips if he was thawing out meat. His phone didn't answer and she hoped he would get the message before she got there, although the prospect of just showing up and claiming access to a bed and his parental care caused her a sneaky delight. The man still owed her, she reckoned, and she didn't mind letting him know it.

6

A couple of hours later she was back in Jackman. In early summer, with lilacs in bloom and most of the winter road grit swept up or washed away, the town had a hopeful glow. Summer camp owners were opening up their getaways, and sports fishing enthusiasts were bringing money into the town.

Simone did not see Gilles's Jeep in the Moose Crossing parking lot, but out of habit she stopped in anyway. She made her way toward the café section, passing fresh racks of moose-themed kiddie pajamas, hunter-orange caps, and bright fishing lures, displayed between cases of liter bottles of Mountain Dew and a box of assorted stove-pipe joints, all laid out for the anticipated summer trade. Knowing the management's relaxed attitude toward dogs, she let Ivy follow her in.

The collection of geezers around the coffeepot was not much smaller than in winter. Two of them were stabbing ineffectually at their smart phones, their expressions suggesting that the phone might bite back at them at any moment. Ivy aimed herself directly at the table, certain of good floor cleanings and maybe even a direct handout. There was no sign of Gilles, but Simone knew most of these people and figured she could afford a few minutes to answer the usual questions about her love life. Telling them all to piss off and mind their own business was part of the game. She was getting an update on Gilles's movements ("hasn't been in here for days—reckon him and Jocelyne are up to the house") when she realized that one of them—an Ivan, maybe, or was he a Vaughn?—was raising his voice and demanding she "get that damn dog out of here." Taken aback, Simone thought he had mistaken Ivy's quest for attention and dropped food for aggression.

"It's okay, she's super friendly," Simone tried to explain. "She's just looking for treats."

"You can't trust them pit bulls," Vaughn, or Ivan, was claiming loudly. "They'll turn on you faster'n you can say knife."

Simone suppressed the urge to call him a prejudiced idiot and went for the reasonable response, offering the suggestions that this was not really true, it was really all about how you raise a dog, and that Labradors were responsible for more dog bites than pit bulls, but she didn't get a chance to finish a sentence as support for the blowhard was coming from his wife, Simone supposed, across the table. She was repeating more stupid bromides about inbred aggression, and Simone had had enough.

"That's the nicest dog any of you will ever be lucky enough to know," she said, directly eyeing the complacent pair, settled happily in their superior knowledge. "The one thing you can count on from her sort is loyalty and—" She was cut short in her efforts to explain Ivy's qualities by the first of her accusers.

"They've got jaws that lock. Can't pry them open once they've gotten a hold on you," he was telling the rest of the bunch.

"Yeah, right, and white men can't jump," was Simone's reply, over her shoulder as she and Ivy headed out the door. She had the satisfaction of realizing that none of them got the reference or had any idea what she was talking about. No wonder, she reflected, they're too fucking stupid to get past dumb stereotypes anyway. Why would they be able to recognize a sweet dog when they met one? You'd think that educated people who had spent their lives in a world with access to information would be able to come up with more than a bunch of silly platitudes.

She took a moment to give Ivy an extra ear-pull. "Don't worry, Fats," she said as Ivy took advantage of her lowered guard and embarked on a thorough face wash for Simone. "I still love you."

Hearing herself say this surprised her. She wasn't sure she had ever said that to another being—other than Mattie, maybe, but that was different—and it took her a moment to swallow the lump that had appeared in her throat. She shook off the feeling and started the truck.

"Let's go see if Gilles has any real food for us," she said. "Who needs these assholes, anyway?"

As it turned out, Gilles was expecting her, and Jocelyne was indeed "up to the house" with him. Gilles was cleaning a net full of small brook trout and seemed genuinely relaxed and pleased to see her. Simone grabbed Ivy before she could make any moves on the fish guts.

"Where'd you get them?" she asked.

"East Pond. The usual spot. Jos and I just got back. Couldn't pull them in fast enough."

Simone was reminded of days when she was a kid, fishing with Gilles on his favorite pond. Maybe they should try for a spell on a pond tomorrow, and she could ask him about Robert's inspection and the wrap-up of Serge's season. She would try the idea on him later.

"Cool," she said, checking out the little fish. "Ivy was hoping for meat, but they look great to me."

Gilles referred her to Jocelyne, who was in the house and had some chicken giblets saved for Ivy. Simone got the beer and groceries out of the truck and went in search of Jocelyne. It looked like a decent evening ahead.

Over pan-fried trout and carrots, eased by beer and a bottle of wine that Jocelyne had at the ready (that's an upgrade, Simone acknowledged—with Gilles alone it was only ever beer), they agreed to Simone's suggestion for a day's fishing before the conversation inevitably turned to the events following Jean-Yves's death. Neither Gilles nor Jocelyne had reason, at this point, to doubt that it had been anything but an accident. They went back over that day and the busy ones that had followed. When the conversation turned to Jean-Yves's family and how they were coping, and then to Mattie, Simone claimed the need for sleep. She did not want to get too near to her recent discoveries until she had first picked them all apart with Serge. As she turned in, she felt more at ease with her father than she could remember. The prospect of a fishing trip with him was, in anticipation, a welcome thought.

With a whole day in hand, there was no need to hurry the next day along. Gilles vanished, wrenches in hand, under the Jeep and left Simone to clean up breakfast and chat with Jocelyne. The domestic arrangements between her father and Jocelyne were not clear. The shared bedroom, the toothbrushes in the rudimentary bathroom told one story, but Jocelyne described a busy life in town and visiting her kids, who were spread around Maine and on the West Coast, that clearly did not involve

Gilles. She seemed more interested in Simone's life than in describing her own. To Simone's relief, she left untouched the topic of her employment status, asking instead about "that handsome fellow at the border." Fair game, Simone thought. She described the brief meeting in Liberty but had nothing to offer when Jocelyne asked her what moves she had made since then.

"Haven't talked to him or anything," she confessed. "I mean, he has my number if he wants to contact me."

"Oh, come on, girl," was Jocelyne's exasperated response. "The guy gave you a puppy, for God's sake. In my book, that's huge. And you gotta admit," she went on, looking over at Ivy's recumbent form, "he got the perfect dog for you. I think that deserves something."

Getting no reply from Simone, she plowed on.

"You know, he's a good one, and they're making them better all the time. Your generation of guys was raised with different views of women."

"Well," Simone said, "Ivy is pretty cool. I'll be up there tomorrow."

"So, did you tell him that?" Jocelyne asked.

"Nah—but he's there a lot. If he is, I'll see him, and if not…" Simone realized she had not given the subject adequate thought, and had probably just assumed that Steve would be his usual pleasant, present self when she went through the crossing.

Jocelyne seemed satisfied that she had at least prodded Simone on the matter. Gilles appeared from under the Jeep with the report that gear and canoe were ready and they should go get some fish. Simone flashed her current license for him to see.

"Be prepared, like they tell you," she said, to her father's approving smile.

East Pond was reached down a rutted track and required some manhandling of canoe and gear to get everything over logs and rocks that kept the unknowing from accessing the water. True to its form, it was edged on one side by a steep, rocky shore with spruce and cedar growing right to the water line. On the opposite side, a shallow, marshy expanse offered breeding and spawning opportunities for any number of waterfowl and fish. It was not uncommon to find herons, ducks of all kinds, loons, and even grebes within one good day on the pond.

Dangling worms off the same old equipment she had used as a kid, Simone was soon pulling in nine-inch brookies. The limit on the pond was three per person, and within a couple of hours, six pretty fish lay in the bottom of the boat. Simone assured her father that she could handle fresh trout two days in a row, and, anxious not to miss the chance to talk to him now that the focus was off catching fish, suggested paddling over to the marshy opposite side of the pond. A beaver dam at the outlet was fun to check out, and moose were common there. They tucked the evening's supper into the cooler of ice and took up familiar paddle positions, with Simone in the bow where she had learned the art, Gilles in the stern. The ability to move a canoe—in this case a slender, somewhat tippy boat whose shape reflected ancient native boat-building skills, rather than the fat, slow rubber duckies favored by the whitewater yahoos—efficiently and silently through almost any water was a skill she cherished. They slid across the pond to the grassy edge and nudged the canoe into the shallows, where it sat peacefully in the still water. She hated to break the calm, but she wanted to know what Gilles could tell her about the LePages, if anything.

It seemed easier to start the conversation where they had left it weeks ago.

"So, LePages," she started. "They selling drugs, or what?" That didn't seem enough of an opener, so she went on.

"Those two next to Serge's. You think they could be up to anything like that?"

Gilles response was immediate.

"Christ, no. They haven't got the balls or the brains. Their confounded uncle is the big guy. Benoit LePage. What a horse's ass he was in school. Year or two younger than me, but mean as a snake even then. I think he gave the sugar business to his nephews to keep them out of his way. Why do you ask?" "They're up to something." Simone had to admit this much. "There's something weird about their sugar operation but that's as much as I can say. MOMP would kill me for spreading gossip."

"Well, nothing would surprise me about anyone in that family. Big Benoit is for sure trying to play in the major leagues. Runs that hideous Hummer through Jackman like he's a big shot, but I stopped having anything to do with him a while ago. Nasty bastard. I'm sorry I ever messed with him." Gilles seemed ready to expand on his severed relationship with his former pill pusher, but Simone moved to keep him on track.

"So the boys and their maple business. Did anything happen there after I left?"

Gilles took a while to think about that. "Nothing I can think of. They were around. Serge and I wrapped things up right after you left. It got too warm and the sap was going off and, to be honest, we had had it up there. Serge needed to get home."

He passed half a candy bar on the tip of his paddle to where Simone could reach it. She tried another question.

"Was Tommy there the whole time? I mean, did you see either of them leave?"

"Couldn't say. You can't really see their yard from Serge's. I know they only had the one truck there and I can't say I ever saw it move." He paused to eat chocolate and added, "I can't imagine they're mixed up in whatever their uncle is doing. I wouldn't trust them with anything important and I bet he wouldn't either. I think that the family must be hoping that they can make the sugar business work so they don't have to support them. They grew up there so at least they know how to tap trees."

So is that the story? Simone wondered. They have to make the maple business work so the family will let them keep it? The drug option wouldn't have explained their unrealistic yields anyway.

"How did the inspection go?" she asked Gilles. "Did Robert say anything about them?"

"Nice young man," was Gilles's response. "He seemed a bit stressed, poor kid, but he did a good job. He liked your records!"

"Cool. He can thank me when I see him. Did he say how the LePage inspection had gone?"

"Not really. He was pretty mum about them, but he did get Serge to show him trees up along their top line. I guess he didn't get a lot of cooperation from them. Come to think of it, he did say they had made a lot of syrup early on. He seemed surprised that we hadn't."

"Hmm. Well, like I said, there's something weird there. That's why I'm meeting Serge at the camp tomorrow."

"Hope you figure out whatever it is," Gilles said. "There's a lot of unhappiness up there right now."

He seemed to want to return to an earlier topic, and stared at the water for a while before getting to his point.

"You know, you were right. About Jos. That whole thing with, you know, the pills and shit. She's a lot better than that."

"Duh," Simone answered before she could stop herself and come up with a nicer reaction. She joined Gilles in examining the water. "Glad you figured that out. She seems to be willing to give you a break."

"Yeah. Like I said, she's better than me in a ton of ways. My job to try harder, I guess."

"Baby steps!" Simone counseled, and they both laughed. They studied the water silently until a shadow caught both their eyes. Looking up they spotted a mature bald eagle cruising over the pond, white tail and head catching the light as it turned slowly on the air currents. Simone could never watch this spectacle without singing 'making lazy circles in the sky' to herself. She could sit there forever, watching and listening to the wilderness.

Gilles was commenting on the big raptor.

"They're everywhere now," he said. "When you were a kid they were still trying to get them established along the coast. Now we have nests on half the ponds up here. They're giving the loons a hard time, Penny tells me." He was quoting his neighbor in Jackman, a retired field biologist for the state Fish and Wildlife department. Win one, lose one, reflected Simone. She hoped that someone was watching out for the loons, possibly the most beautiful bird she knew. Without their splendid presence and their strange, complex language, she wasn't sure she would want to live in Maine.

"Let's get these fish home before the ice melts," Gilles said, prompting them back into action. They paddled quietly across the pond, swatting mosquitoes as they neared the shore. As they hauled the canoe back to its trailer and loaded gear and fish into the Jeep, swarms of blackflies assaulted them, getting in their eyes and under their hats.

"Miserable bastards," Gilles said, reaching for the toxic DEET-laced spray he loved. Simone refused to use the stuff and fled for the safety of the closed Jeep.

"Keeps the tourists out," she said, repeating the locals' favorite excuse for putting up with the pestilence. You got used to them after a while. Newbies to the state would swell up in huge welts when bitten, but the well-acclimated only had to suffer a maddening itch for an hour or two, after which a small red dot was the only evidence of attack.

They bumped their way out of the woods and back to the cabin. Supper of trout and salad. Not a bad way to live, they all agreed.

* * *

Simone approached the crossing at Saint-Zacharie the next morning with some trepidation. She wanted Steve to be there but felt foolish for not having told him she was coming. With a mixture of disappointment and relief that she found the backup lady officer on duty. Despite her best efforts to appear casual and unconcerned, she could not stop herself from asking whether Officer Haskell was around.

"Back tomorrow. His shift starts eight a.m.," she was told. Simone acknowledged the information with a nonchalant nod, but she was evidently not fooling anyone.

"I'll tell him you came through," said the officer, whose badge identified her as a member of the Willette clan. Simone thanked her, and added, now that the game was up, "We'll be here at least until the Braisethwaite pickup is done."

Officer Willette clearly had her finger on the pulse of maple camp activity. "Right, she said. "Sugar Shack is due in too, as far as I know."

Simone found Serge puttering in his camp, tidying odds and ends of line paraphernalia into boxes and putting up new hooks for whatever didn't fit into a box. It was a clear, bright June day with blackflies as thick as bonfire smoke. Head-net time, thought Simone. Her pressing need was to get Serge up to the broken tree and show him the axe cuts. Then she would tell him of Mattie's suspicions and what she had found in the MOMP files, confidentiality rules be damned. She had to share what she knew with someone she trusted. As soon as the basic greetings were over and Ivy had been congratulated on her considerable increase in size, Simone addressed her uncle.

"Hey. Serge. Stop with the messing around there. I need you to come up the road with me. Like, now."

He caught the urgency in her voice and put down his tools.

"What's up? Something bothering you?" he asked.

"It's that fucking tree, where Jean-Yves died. I need you to see it. Have you been up there lately?"

"Not since we pulled taps out—it was pissing rain. Why? Something happened I don't know about?" Serge was heading for the ATV anyway. "Come on. Whatever it is, you can show me."

Simone bundled a protesting Ivy into the camp. "Sorry, babe," she said. "This one is just your uncle and me. Look after the camp. We won't be gone long."

They climbed easily up the now-firm track to the turn, and stopped when Simone tapped Serge on the shoulder as they approached the fallen birch. She wanted Serge to see it all without her prompting, wanting to get his unprepped reaction. When he pulled himself off the ATV she just looked in the direction of the tree and waited to see what he made of it. She watched as his eye followed the trunk back to the break, still as she had found it. He rubbed the hacked edge of the broken trunk and then stood straight, now running his eye to the cable that still draped across the track.

"*Tab-er-NAK*," she heard him say softly to himself.

She had never heard him use the old Quebecois profanity before—it was not thrown around as casually as its English counterparts.

"*Ces maudits bâtards*," he added.

Without looking at Simone, he picked up the cable and ran his hand along it until he came to where it was looped around the broken birch. His hand then explored the trunk below the cable. Finding nothing, he straightened his back to examine the second trunk, still standing behind the hacked stump. Knowing that he had seen what she had seen, Simone stepped toward him.

"There was a tie-back to that trunk, right?" she asked him, keeping her voice low so as not to disrupt his thought process.

"*Oui*. You helped me put it there." He was silent for a while, then unexpectedly reached an arm out to encircle Simone's shoulders. "*Criss,*" he muttered, "*et calvaire.*"

Simone reached into the pocket of her jeans and pulled out the scrap of pink flagging tape she had found before.

"This was on the ground when I came up here. They must have dropped it." She knew that Serge already grasped that the tree had been cut and the support wire removed. She knew, too, that he would recognize the ribbon and the significance of its absence.

He took it from her and held it.

"We put meters of it on that cable," he said. "He might have seen it…"

He didn't finish his sentence. Without another word he pulled Simone toward him and they stood looking at what they both now knew was the result of deliberate, evil action.

"When did you find this?" Serge wanted to know.

"Week ago. You were in New Hampshire. I had to get back to work." She didn't want Serge to think she had been sitting on this discovery for days for no reason, as if there was no urgency to it.

"There's something else. A lot, actually. I need to tell you what I have figured out."

She leaned against him and shuddered, feeling huge relief at having split her burden into two.

"Let's go back to camp."

He turned the ATV round and slowly let it coast down to the camp yard.

Ivy was quick to recognize their mood. As Serge opened two beers and set them on the table, she nudged Simone with an anxious snout.

"Go lie down. Serge and I have to talk." Simone tried to push her toward the blankets by the now cold woodstove, but Ivy was having none of it. With a deep sigh and an apologetic wag of her tail, she took up her post as protector, getting as much of herself on Simone's feet as would fit.

Serge waited before he prompted Simone.

"What else?" he asked eventually.

Once she got started, Simone could not stop, and she delivered the whole story, from Mattie's first text to the weird and inexplicable high production numbers that the LePage boys had achieved that season. Serge listened as she described Mattie's insistence that the accident was no accident, her discovery of the tree that had been felled, and her inability to figure out why in hell anyone would do that or what it was that Mattie had seen or suspected, and then her sense that the yield numbers were wrong and her decision that while Serge was out of reach she could, at least, look into their numbers. She felt her narrative was running off the track, but Serge was following it all, rubbing his fingers together as he listened to her. When she was finally out of information about her discoveries, she paused and looked at him.

"I just don't understand," she finished. "What the fuck is going on? I mean, what did Mattie and Jean-Yves do? I can't even begin to think that those two LePage jack-asses could have meant for Jean-Yves to run into that cable, but what other explanation is there?"

Serge reached one hand over and covered hers.

"Something bad has happened here," he said, "and it's not your job to find out how or why it happened. We need to get that game warden back here and tell him everything you told me. He will know what to do next. It's late on a Sunday right now, but first thing tomorrow, we get hold of him, okay? Now we need food and a night's sleep."

They ate in silence, but as they cleared dishes and finished another couple of beers, Serge was thinking about Mattie.

"You know, he hasn't been as disturbed as this since he was in middle school. This thing has scared the lights out of him. It's more than just losing his friend, horrible as that is. He knows there's something dangerous going on. You were right to believe him."

"Are the LePage boys in camp now?" Simone asked. "The lady at the border said that Sugar Shack trucks were coming in this week too." Another thought occurred to her. "How come they went to the Sugar Shack people anyway? I thought they sold to Braisethwaites, like you."

"Ah. That's a story." Serge was glad of a change of topic and described his visit to the big maple syrup buyer in New Hampshire.

"I spent a good deal of time—and trouble—with those guys. They are complaining that the price of syrup is falling and they don't want to pick up small loads any more. I had to remind them, repeatedly, of how long I have been a good producer for them, and that I invested in new trees just for them. Had to point out that I'm making high grade syrup, like most everyone up here, but still. Seems like the Sugar Shack has picked up a few camps that Braisethwaites has dropped but if they can't make Grade A organic syrup, or enough of it, they'll have to sell into the Canadian conventional market—and then they are really screwed."

There was little else to do until morning. Simone spent a night of poor sleep and anxious anticipation of the events to come. The relief she felt at having told everything she knew to Serge was coupled with the realization that this was no longer her weird and unexposed secret. She had set in motion events that she would not control, starting with the involvement of the game warden the next day.

* * *

When the night was finally over, Serge took his truck to within phone reception to call the wardens' service. Needing something to do, Simone loaded Ivy onto the tool box rack on the back of the ATV for one more look at the top of the LePage sugar bush. Mattie and Jean-Yves had seen something up there. Maybe she could see it too.

Ivy protested the uncomfortable ride, so at the top of the rise, Simone stopped to let her off.

"Okay, blue eyes," she said. "Do it your way, but keep up. We need to get back to help Serge."

Ivy bounced alongside the ATV, barking gleefully, despite Simone's admonitions. Where the track petered out just past the pump house, she turned the ATV around and cut the engine.

"Shush, fool," she commanded the excited dog. "You'll scare the squirrels."

She headed straight down the slope below the road, into the LePage trees, looking around her for anything that could be a clue to what the boys had seen. The familiar LePage lines, some sagging and clogged with the grime that developed in stagnant sap, were all she could find. Their taps had been pulled and hung from the lines on their connecting "drops." Engrossed in her examination of the trees, it took her a while to realize that Ivy was behaving strangely. She had pushed past Simone and

116

into the woods a few yards, where she had taken up a prize-fighter stance and was generating a peculiarly menacing low growl. Simone had never heard anything but grunting noises and happy barking from her, and was thinking a bear was nearby when she realized what was putting Ivy's hackles up. Partially obscured by a large tree, Tommy LePage was visible some fifty yards beyond Ivy, with an odd-looking gadget in his hands. It took her a moment to understand what he was holding. Fuck—that's not line-mending gear, she realized. That's a fucking crossbow. And he was aiming it at her.

Before she could react, Ivy had made a decision, hurling herself in the general direction of the LePage guy, her growls having evolved into loud, angry barking. A nanosecond later, Simone heard a click, followed by a shriek from Ivy, who had turned from a directed missile into a twisted, jerking form in the leaves in front of Simone. Her mind instantly cleared of any thought except for her dog. Blood was pouring from somewhere under Ivy's neck, turning the leaves around her red. Simone stumbled toward her, pulling off her jacket, ready to scoop up her pet, noticing as she did that there was something dreadfully wrong with Ivy's face. Her bottom jaw seemed to be in the wrong place and blood was gushing from her mouth to mix with the flow from her neck. She reached Ivy, who was struggling to get to her feet, yelping in pain and fear as she did.

"It's okay, it's okay, I've got you." She tried to calm the panicked dog. One small part of her mind was on the lookout for more danger, but the trees above them were quiet. We have to get out of here, was all she could think. She got the whole bloody bundle of dog and jacket into her arms and back to the trail where the ATV, mercifully pointed toward home, was waiting. Frantically trying to stuff parts of her jacket into wherever the blood was coming from, Simone got the ATV running and, one arm holding onto Ivy, who by now was limp and apparently in shock, she drove, shaking, down the hill to the camp.

In her head, one track was running a loop of invective—that scum-sucker fucking shot my dog, that fucking bastard, bastard, bastard—while another track was forming a plan. Saint-Georges had an excellent vet practice, but it would take an hour to get there and Ivy seemed to be bleeding too heavily to make the trip without some attention. Simone's knowledge of emergency first aid was rudimentary, but surely stopping the bleeding was the first priority. She was making a quick inventory of towels and bandages that she could lay hands on, planning the moves that would get her and Ivy onto the road in the least possible time. Finally reaching the camp yard, she was taken aback to find a group of people watching her chaotic arrival.

Shouting for help, she half fell off the ATV, clutching the bleeding, whimpering dog. She was incoherent, explanation for what had occurred being far too complicated when all she needed was help.

"He shot Ivy. She's really hurt. I don't want her to die. I have to get her to the vet." She was about to start again, frantic to generate the responses she needed, when she felt a large presence in front of her. She looked up to find Pierre Bolduc, who had been leaning against his enormous pickup, gently taking Ivy out of her arms, mindless of the blood that was now spreading over the front of his shirt. Serge was next, demanding to know what had happened. She took a breath and tried to explain.

"I don't know. We were up by the pump house. Tommy LePage was up there. Ivy sort of ran at him. He had a crossbow and he shot her. I have no damn idea where he went. I think he took off. I have to get her to the vet—she's bleeding really badly."

Another figure appeared, a familiar outline in a Fisheries and Wildlife Department uniform. Of course. The game warden, Leonard Lewey. Whatever he thought he had come to investigate, he now had a new problem, and he appeared to think that saving an injured dog was the first priority. He was giving orders, directing Pierre to set the dog on the truck tail gate and cautiously unwrapping Simone's coat from around her.

"I can try to stop the bleeding. I need clean padding. What have you got we can pack this with?" he asked, calm and professional and blessedly knowledgeable.

"Padding, right, I've got that," Simone responded. The plan she had made on the way down the trail kicked in, and in a few short strides she was in the camp, pulling towels out of the trunk, a large box of maxipads from under the bathroom sink, and some not-so-clean ace bandages from a shelf over the table. Never knew I'd be glad I have these things, she thought, as she handed pads to the warden. He packed them in a half circle around Ivy's chest, wrapping them tightly against her with the old bandage. Then he turned to her face. Blood was pouring from her mouth and part of her bottom jaw was not where it ought to be. Her tongue was flapping as she tried to cope with the blood running into her mouth—or running out of it, it was hard to tell. The warden wrapped a towel loosely round her jaw and secured it with more bandage.

"Is she...?" Simone hardly dare ask what she wanted to know. The misshapen face was looking at her and, miracle of miracles, the very tip of Ivy's tail gave a hesitant quiver.

"I don't know about her jaw. Looks sort of shattered to me. She's shot through the shoulder, but I don't think it got her lungs. The blood in her mouth is from her jaw—she's not coughing blood. You should get going."

Simone looked around for Serge. Of course, he had been right there passing stuff to Lewey. Pierre Bolduc was piling towels on her passenger seat and preparing to load the suffering dog onto them. Simone turned to Serge.

"That bastard Tommy is up there somewhere. Tell the warden. We walked down into their trees below the pump house. Ivy was barking. He must have heard us coming. I think he was waiting for us. He had one of those little hand-held crossbows." She looked around at the party she had crashed with the bleeding dog, and recognized the Braisethwaites truck backed up to the syrup barrels, which the driver was preparing to load.

"You need to go deal with all this," she told Serge. "I'm going to the vet in Saint-Georges. I'll call Marie Noëlle when I get there, so you should let her know I'm heading her way."

"Go carefully," he said. "A few minutes won't make a difference, but going off the road will."

He gestured at the Warden Service truck. "And thank God the warden is here. He saw all this. I'll talk to him, try to go find out what he's going to do." Serge rubbed a hand over his face and glanced at the confused-looking Braisethwaites driver.

"Shit," he added, "I need to go take care of this guy. He'll want to get back across the border before it closes tonight."

"Go," Simone said. As she slid into the truck, where Ivy was quivering pitifully beside her, Pierre appeared by her window.

"Do you want me to drive you?" he asked.

"No, no. Stay here and help Serge. I'll be fine."

She drove out, praying as she tried to avoid bumps and keep the ride smooth.

"Please live. Please, please, don't you die too."

The routine phone check-in at the Canadian border trailer, usually a brief stop not worth killing an engine for, was interminable, but she thanked her gods when Steve's face emerged from his office as she slowed to a halt at the US post. The "get over here" gesture from Simone squelched his initially cautious approach.

"Oh, good lord, what happened?" He reached in to touch Ivy's limp form.

"She got shot. Those LePage bastards are out to get us. I need to tell you, but I have to get her to a vet." Encouraged by his concerned face, she said, "Do us a favor? Call the vet clinic in Saint-Georges up by the cathedral. Tell them to be ready. I'll be there as soon as I can."

He made no response other than a quick "You got it," and motioned her to get going. Just be here when I get back, Simone thought, wondering as she drove off why the hell she hadn't said that out loud.

* * *

It was afternoon before the verdict came from the vet. Simone sat with knots in her guts while Ivy was sedated, X rayed and diagnosed. The elderly vet, whose qualifications (vet school in Montreal and, of all places, Tennessee) Simone now knew intimately, having read and reread the certificates on the wall, had hopeful news.

"That's about the strangest set of injuries I have seen in a while," he said. "Your dog got her face in the way of whatever shot her. She has a busted-up lower jaw and damage to her shoulder, but we can stick her back together for you. I don't think it's as bad as it looked. She lost a lot of blood, but she is a big strong girl and she'll be all right once we get some new blood into her." Simone went on looking at her hands, afraid of his sympathy.

"It's okay," he assured her. "I'm good at this. Did lots of woodworking with my dad when I was a kid. It's just carpentry."

He got a grateful half smile from Simone and went on. "We'll need to keep her overnight at least. Call me in the morning and I'll let you know how she is."

Finding words a problem, Simone nodded and mumbled thanks and promises to be back the next day.

* * *

Pierre Bolduc, blessedly equipped with brains, mobility, and a cell phone, had alerted Marie-Noëlle, and she and Mattie were waiting for Simone. A huge laundry load and some food later, still shaken but ready to face the consequences of the day's new trauma, Simone sat beside Mattie on the sofa, ignoring his attempts to withdraw.

"Matts, look at me. You have to do this. You were right. Those LePage assholes are up to something and you have to tell me what you know. We have to stop them."

She got little more than an awkward squirm from her cousin, but he stayed put on the sofa after glancing briefly at his grandmother, who was clinking dishes at the sink. Simone sensed an advantage.

"It's okay," she assured him. "You can talk to me. Mémère's up to speed. She knows everything I know and Serge does too. Nobody is going to blame you."

"What was it that kicked them off?" she asked Mattie. "What did you and Jean-Yves find that turned them into—?" She was going to say "killers," but dropped back to "total assholes."

Mattie picked up his well-worn Rubik's Cube and started clicking the squares. With some effort, speaking directly to his knees, he said, "It's their lower line. They've got a tube there that they don't need for sap collection. We sort of followed it to see where it was coming from."

Their lower line, thought Simone. Line A. And I have only been looking at the top one, Line B, where the trap that killed Jean-Yves was set.

"So then what? What did you find?" she prompted, trying to keep the information coming.

Mattie's manipulation of the cube gathered speed.

"Nothing," he admitted. "Bernard saw us and he was really mad. He had a pistol crossbow, a good one, a Prophecy." Even under threat he had collected gadget details. He struggled on, the end in sight. "He told us he could kill us and he'd do it if we told anyone anything. Jean-Yves wasn't scared. He told him to *va chier*."

"So then what happened?" "Nothing really. I don't think he wanted to shoot us, not then, anyway. But he was real pissed off. We just left, climbed up to Uncle Serge's road and went home. We were going to tell you about it when you came back but…" He couldn't finish the sentence. They both knew what had happened to silence him.

"Oh shit, Matts, it's all my fault. I asked you to check them out. I am so sorry."

The information loop had come full circle. She had casually asked two boys who knew no filter, who would do anything they did to the maximum without thought of consequences, to spy on dangerous people, and now one was dead and the other a terrified wreck.

"I'm so sorry," she repeated. "But I'll get them. I promise."

They sat on the sofa in silence. I have to get back there, Simone thought. I know what I'm looking for now. She was juggling thoughts of Ivy with plans to get back to camp and put an end to this nightmare, whatever the consequences, when the phone rang.

"It's Serge," Marie-Noëlle reported. "He says he is stuck in camp tonight and will be here tomorrow. He wants to talk to you."

Simone grabbed the phone.

"Serge, listen. I know what we have to do. Stay there. I'll be there in two days"

The memory of him standing there with the game warden (had that been only earlier this same day?) came back to her.

"What happened? Did they find Tommy? What's going on?"

"Out of my hands," was Serge's response. "Lewey called in state cops. They found the LePages, but the cops didn't seem to think it was all a big deal. How's Ivy? She going to be okay?" he added.

"Looks like it. I have to get her in the morning. But stay where you are. Wait for me to get there, okay?"

With a promise to do just that from Serge, she hung up and turned back to Mattie. If the cops weren't going to take the LePages seriously, she was going to have to do it.

"Matts," she said. "I have to go back to Serge's camp. I'm going to find out what they were up to. But you have to take care of Ivy for me. She loves you and she's going to need a lot of looking after. Can you do that?"

For the first time in so very long, a look that came close to happiness came over Mattie's face. He nodded vigorously, and looked directly at Simone. *I love her too,* was his silent assurance

Ignoring the vet's request that she call, Simone was on the doorstep well before office hours began. When doors opened to an impatient client, the staff were unfazed but firm. She would have to wait to talk to the vet until after morning surgery hours.

To keep herself busy while the hours passed, she set off to buy soft food that she supposed Ivy was going to need. Finding the best food meant shopping at the Père Nature store, where she filled a cart with every mushy delicacy she could find. With another hour to waste, she worked off nervous energy along the riverside path and the footbridges over the Chaudière River.

Ivy, when she was finally allowed to see her, was a strange sight. Her lower jaw was encased in weird scaffolding, pins and wires protruding from all sides. Her left front end was shaved to smooth pink skin, and an impressive line of thick metal staples, holding a fat ridge of skin together, ran from her neck to right behind her left elbow.

"So here's what we've done," the vet was explaining. "We've wired her jaw back to where it ought to be. She's missing a few teeth, but she had plenty to spare. She won't be able to chew anything hard for a while, but when it all heals up she'll be good as new—apart from a lopsided smile. As for her shoulder, her scapula was broken but her face must have slowed the bolt, 'cause it's not that bad. Nicked a blood vessel, which made a mess, but we fixed that and pinned the bone and that should all heal up too."

"Can I take her home?" was Simone's anxious question. Visions of enormous vet bills conflicted with a desire to have the very best care for Ivy.

"Well. She had a good night. She'll be okay as long as you can watch her. She needs rest and nursing."

Simone launched into a description of her cousin, her desire to explain just how well Mattie would look after Ivy in some conflict with a fear that she was making him sound weirder than was fair. Her pleas for Ivy's release appeared to sway the vet. He took a long look at Ivy, who looked lovingly back at him. He ran a hand over her rump.

"She's a sweetheart," he said. "Most dogs hate me but she's just all love and forgiveness. Lesson for us all."

Ivy's tail was back to full operating capacity. Simone carried the wobbly but seemingly undaunted dog out to her truck. A bag of medical supplies—pain killers, antibiotics, a package of wound-care bottles and syringes, plus detailed instructions on keeping the jaw repair clean and stable—was provided, and with the promise that she would have Ivy back at the clinic in two days, Simone turned back toward Saint-Prosper.

"Stupid damn pit bull," Simone told her. "What you want to go lunging at jerks in the woods for?"

She didn't know when she had ever felt so grateful—for the dog who had quite literally taken a bullet, or at least a bolt, for her, for the vet who had mended and understood her, and for the chance to give her to Mattie to care for. The feeling did little to lessen the guilt she knew she would carry forever, but she felt renewed determination to uncover all the information possible on the scum, and their actions, that had caused all this harm in good people's lives. She wanted them permanently removed from any possibility of ever causing such pain again.

* * *

One more night in Saint-Prosper. Simone was impatient to get back to Serge, but she needed to settle Ivy in and go over nursing care with Mattie. There was no question that she would get the most detailed and careful care that any misbegotten pit bull had ever received. Mattie and Marie-Noëlle were instructed to take her for her doctor's appointment in two days if Simone wasn't back. At the end of the day, with some sense that things were getting better, or at least better understood, Simone tucked Ivy up on the end of Mattie's bed and got the best night's sleep she'd had for a while.

7

A sense of calm descended over Simone as she headed once more for the Saint-Zacharie border crossing. She knew she had to find out exactly what the boys had seen, and she knew that it would lead to some sort of conclusion. Those scumbags had something to hide, and she would find out what that was. I'll get those fuckers was the one thought that drove her.

First, though, she had to see Steve. Not had to, she thought. Wanted to. Was even anxious to. She was aware that her automatic defense system was down and failing to emit even weak warning signals. Jocelyne's comments appeared to have disabled it beyond repair.

She had to wait while he checked papers, but he caught her eye as he entered her passport into his database and her heart gave a small bump. The bathroom offered a convenient brief retreat, and she emerged to find him eagerly asking for news of Ivy's status.

"I'm an idiot," Simone had to confess. "I could have texted you. Yesterday was pretty much a blur. But she's going to be okay. The vet was all primed and ready when we got there—thank you so much. I've left her with Mattie. They are going to get some quality sofa time together."

She felt the need to explain her prompt return to the camps, but was unsure how much of the LePage malfeasance was appropriate for discussion with an officer of the law. She could find out from Serge what had gone down, but saw no harm in trying a simple question.

"What happened after I left? Did anyone catch that son of a bitch?"

"Ongoing investigation," was all she got, and she could tell from his face that he wasn't going to say any more. Better not to get into Mattie's suspicions, she figured. She didn't want anyone telling her that it was not her job to investigate whatever shit the LePages had gotten up to. She went back to Mattie and Ivy, happy to let him know that his puppy gift was now bringing solace to her unhappy cousin.

"I'm really glad," he said. "I thought she was kind of special even as a pup."

Simone was making her way back to the truck when Jocelyne's voice came into her head. She turned back and managed to look into Steve's eyes.

"When this shit all dies down, maybe you could come take her for a walk with me," she said, surprising herself with such a direct invitation. "My mom keeps telling me that the Hills to Sea trail from Unity is worth exploring. Ivy's going to need some nice slow walks as she gets better."

"You bet," was his response. "We should introduce her to my dad's cows—see what she thinks of them."

She left with a bland explanation that she was going to check on Serge and see whether he was cool with leaving the camp—that and a promise to get together in Liberty when life returned to something near normal.

Serge was waiting, looking worn and sad, and Simone was struck by the realization of how much he meant to her. His quiet, skilled, practical self had been a constant throughout her bumpy childhood, and the guilt she felt at the misery she had brought upon Mattie transferred itself momentarily onto her uncle. No way out but straight ahead, she told herself. We have to figure out what these shitheads were up to. Then maybe we can nail them with something more than suspicions, and bring some peace to us all.

"Come on," she said. "Coffee and talk. I need to know what happened yesterday and I have new stuff to tell you. But you should know that Ivy will be okay and she is looking after Mattie. I think he'll be okay too."

Serge ran an exhausted hand through his hair. Something about his air of defeat hit Simone right under her ribs.

"Oh God, *mon oncle*, I am so sorry. Are you going to be okay?" she asked.

He gave her a brief smile.

"Sure," he said. "I just want to get home."

The exploration of the LePage lines would have to wait until she had infused some life into Serge. With the box of muffins that the prescient

Marie-Noëlle had handed her under one arm and her uncle's elbow under the other, she directed them both into the camp and fired up the coffeemaker. Never one to welcome opportunities for physical contact, she nonetheless pushed Serge into a chair and squeezed the top of his shoulders through his shirt.

"Listen," she said. "I talked to Mattie, and he talked to me. I've left Ivy with him and they're both going to be okay. But we have to find out what kicked this whole thing off. I'm betting the cops aren't going to do it."

She got a sigh from Serge.

"State cop came up after you left," he said. "He went over and talked to the LePages. I guess that little swine Tommy said he was attacked by a dangerous dog and shot at it in self-defense. Said he was innocently up there shooting squirrels—they chew the lines and he was claiming he gave a damn about their crappy equipment. Anyway, the cop didn't seem to think there was anything wrong with that. Tommy doesn't need any kind of permit for that little pea-shooter he carries, and apparently his hunting license checked out, so I guess that was that."

He paused while Simone put coffee, muffins, butter, and syrup on the table. Get some caffeine and sugar into him and he'll get his fight back, she hoped. She knew that even in his darkest mood he would not resist Marie-Noëlle's baking. She didn't stand much of a chance herself, and four muffins and a lot of butter later she felt they were both ready to move ahead.

"What about the tree—didn't that mean anything to anyone?" she asked him.

"Couldn't get the cop interested," Serge said. "I guess it all sounded too—woodsy."

He struggled to explain why he had failed to engage the policeman in a story about a downed tree and a weeks-old accident that maybe wasn't an accident and had no obvious connection to a seemingly justified act of self-defense.

"Lewey, different story," he said, sounding brighter. "No flies on him. We went back up there after the cop left and he was pretty much horrified, I think. He hadn't seen that the tree was hacked when he first looked at it with Gilles."

Serge paused again, remembering the day that Jean-Yves had died. "I shoulda gone with him. I would have seen that the tree had been messed with. Gilles didn't know about the tie-back and the tape. It didn't look weird to him."

"For chrissake," Simone interrupted. "I should have noticed that. I was with Gilles when we found Jean-Yves. I don't remember seeing anything except his body lying there."

There was silence for a moment.

"It was so—awful," was all she could add.

Serge's silent agreement hung in the air for a while. Simone picked up the coffee mugs and swept muffin crumbs into her hand, checking the impulse to drop them onto the floor for Ivy.

"We've got work to do," she said firmly. "We know what those bastards did to Jean-Yves and now we have to prove it, and figure out why. So here's what Mattie told me. They saw something odd about the LePages' lower sap line and the LePages knew it. That's when they fucked around with the tree—though I am damned if I can figure out what they thought that would get them. Too stupid to think beyond scaring the boys, I guess. Anyway, seems it worked better than they expected, but they've been trying to keep people from looking at their lines ever since. They fed Robert some bullshit when he went for the inspection. You know damn well they were both there and they both speak good English. They were just blowing smoke so he wouldn't get into the woods or ask them a lot of questions."

Serge blamed himself for another missed opportunity. "Same thing that day. I wasn't paying attention when I did the tour. If I had seen all this then, things might have been different."

"Wouldn't have saved Jean-Yves," Simone pointed out.

"True, but if we had been smarter we might have saved you from nearly getting shot."

"Well, we get to thank Ivy for that, and she's going to make it. So now we need to find some answers. Here's what we know," she said. "The LePage sap production numbers are too high. And the boys busted the LePages doing something, and scared those jerks into coming up with a stupid plan to shut them up. Plus they did their best to keep the inspector out of the woods and in the dark. Then I guess they got spooked yesterday when we were all here. Tommy must have seen me head up the track with Ivy and—well, he lost what little mind he has and shot her."

The coffee, the recap of the villainy that had got them to this moment, plus his niece's apparent conviction that there was more they could do were having a bracing effect on Serge.

"Okay. So what are we going to do?" he asked. "What else did Mattie give you?"

"Nothing, just that they are doing something dodgy up there that involves a sap line. It's got to be the explanation for the amount of syrup they are making."

An earlier part of their conversation that morning came back to her.

"Did you tell the game warden about the stuff I found in their records?" she asked. "He should be able to understand that, surely."

"I didn't really," Serge admitted. "Wasn't the moment. He was busy calling in the state cop and checking that idiot's little crossbow. I told him what you told me, but it sounded a bit, you know, complicated. But I got the feeling he's not done. I'm guessing he needs to hear it all from you."

"Well. That was the plan! So now we need to get some on-the-ground evidence. If they are faking syrup numbers we have to be able to find out how."

Serge wanted to check.

"We know they made syrup early, before we were getting any, but there could be a reason for that. Trees don't all behave the same. And their overall numbers are way too high. Obvious answer is they are tapping a bunch of trees that they aren't admitting to."

"Sure but what trees, and where? Even if they are tapping all the undersize trees in their sugar bush they'd have a hard time making up that much sap. And they'd never get away with tapping a lot of new trees outside their lease. The LandWay guy"—she named the management company—"would catch them within one year."

She pulled out her phone and found the picture she had taken of the LePage map. Serge's snort of disgust at the child-like scribble confirmed her view of the thing. They both examined the little screen.

"I guess we could go count taps," Serge said. "Their numbers are vague enough that we might learn something."

"Ugh," was Simone's reaction. "That's a lot of taps to count. I'll do it if we have to, but first we go see what Mattie is talking about—the line the boys spotted. There's nobody over there, right?"

"No—they beat it right after the Sugar Shack left." Serge was making a move, shaking a can of bug spray in preparation for a good dousing.

Simone got up and started hunting through bags in the entryway for head nets and the old, long-sleeved white shirts that she favored over the vile spray for black-fly protection. She found a favorite, secured the wrists with elastic bands, and settled a head net over the collar. Serge was outside, spluttering as he tried to avoid inhaling the fog of insect repellent he had created. Simone accepted a battered cap whose brim he had wetted down with the stuff. A little extra defense won't hurt, as long as it's not all over my skin, she thought.

Bug protection in place, they started toward the LePage camp. The roads were now dry and dusty, the maples in bright, young leaf, and everywhere the sounds and smells of early summer. Before they got out of the camp yard, Serge had an idea. He doubled back and ducked into the camp, reappearing seconds later with two mesh onion bags.

"Fiddleheads," he said. "There are always good ones in that wet ground beyond their camp. Might as well get something good out of going there."

Oh good, he's back, Simone thought. She never knew him to miss a chance to gather fiddleheads for Marie-Noëlle.

The LePage camp was quiet and empty. With the filled barrels gone, its appearance of neglect was even more apparent than it had been when Simone had last seen it. They made their way to the back of the shack, to where the sap lines ran down from the woods and entered the building. Simone was used to looking at different collection setups, and had a decent understanding of how the various vacuum systems worked. Most producers, like Serge, ran dual wet/dry vacuum lines, one for the air and one for the sap. This was an upgrade over a single wet line, as it was more efficient and easier to monitor for leaks. But as far as she knew, LePages still ran single wet lines directly into the camp where the vacuum releasers and storage tanks were located.

With this in mind, she looked again at the LePage lines. The two main lines—B from the top trees, A from the more distant, lower ones—approached the camp from their respective areas of the sugar bush and entered it through a hole in the wall. But what caught her attention, something she had missed when she had taken her first quick look around the camp, was a second line of standard one-inch mainline tubing connected to the wire that supported the A line.

Serge saw the same thing.

"What do they need that second line for since they don't run a dual system?"

"No kidding." Simone stepped up to the hole through which the tubing passed, hoping to learn something about the extra tube's destination, but Serge was already starting up the track that the A line followed.

"Let's see where it comes from. We can get a look inside later if we need to."

The trees that fed the lower line were situated a fair way from the camp. The rough track that it followed was an easy snowmobile ride in winter, but without snow to provide an even surface it was a wet, rutted challenge, crossing swampy ground full of fiddlehead ferns and skunk cabbage. They followed the sap lines for perhaps half a mile, at which point the road swung left and the sap line veered right, rising slightly to an unkempt stand of maples with the familiar web of collection tubing.

Serge and Simone stopped. Question marks hung over them as they looked at the perplexing sight in front of them. The extraneous line that was the object of their curiosity had been attached to the support wire that carried the legitimate sap line all the way from the camp, but at this point it became a mass of loose coils, lying on the ground. It was an enormous length of tubing, connected to nothing at this end, piled haphazardly in front of them.

"What the hell?" they said in unison.

Serge wasn't waiting. He was following the track where it curved left and slightly uphill. Simone followed him, and as they pushed through some scrub and a downed tree they found themselves at a dilapidated, padlocked gate, beyond which a roughly cleared strip of land ran along a sagging wire fence.

"It's the border," Serge announced. "This was a crossing when I was a boy—there was an old power line or something ran in here. It's been closed forever but that's Canada right there."

The ground rose gently away from them beyond the gate, but they could make out a clearing in the trees on the far side of the border strip.

"Do you know where that is?" Simone asked Serge. "What's over there?"

"Well, the other end of the old road is still there. Comes in from the 204 somewhere. I could find it easy enough. But what the hell are they doing with this piece of pipeline?"

"Duh. Running something through it is my guess," Simone offered.

"You don't say," Serge agreed. "But what, and from where?"

"That's the next thing we find out. Come on, we need to get into the camp and see what's on the other end."

They started back down the track. As they passed the coils of tubing Simone stopped and demanded that Serge estimate the length of it while she took photographs. Reaching the swampy area near the camp, Serge flourished his onion bag and started snapping fiddleheads off the bronze crowns of the parent plants.

"Seriously?" she asked. "We're picking fiddleheads?"

"You bet. Come on, pick fast and we'll fill a bag in no time." Catching her exasperation, Serge allowed himself a smile.

"It's still early," he said. "One bag and we're on our way."

Finding it easier to acquiesce, Simone bent to the task, glad that she had worn good rubber boots. The little curled shoots were easy picking, and Serge was right: within minutes they had a respectable harvest and Serge's mood had taken another step forward.

Back in the LePage yard, they went once more to the spot where the sap lines entered the camp. Faced with a solid camp wall, they worked their way around the building, meeting locked doors and shuttered windows. Opportunity presented itself in the form of a lean-to woodshed on one end of the camp. Its door was padlocked but the hinges had disintegrated, and they pried it away from the wall enough to squeeze into the dank shed. An unprotected window offered little resistance to Serge's Leatherman tool, and with only a small struggle they found themselves in an untidy storage area. In the dim light, they made their way past the big evaporator to the back wall, where the sap lines entered. A familiar setup greeted them. The sap lines ran to a vacuum-release tank poised over a steel reservoir. As this filled, sap was pumped to the R/O room, and from there the separated concentrate and the clean filter water were pumped to holding tanks in the attic above them. All as it should be. But what of the extra line? Using the flashlight on her phone, Simone found the line where it entered the camp. It consisted of a short coil tied back to the wall above the entrance hole. Attached to it was a coupling with a shut-off valve, and looped over the hook that held it was a length of flexible tubing with a corresponding coupling.

"So, huh? They're bringing in what here?" Simone asked. "I've seen water lines from wells that look like this, but that's not it."

"They must be running sap in from Canada. What else could it be? Doesn't make a lot of sense though. If they've got spare sap in Canada they could process it there for a lot less trouble. I doubt the price they get here is worth the effort."

"Unless they just need more sap to keep this operation alive," Simone conjectured. "Nobody ever suggested these two would do the smart thing, anyway."

"Come on, let's go see what else we can find." She pulled Serge out into the main body of the camp. A cluttered workbench revealed a rack of shop flashlights, and after testing them all they found one with a working battery. Serge set out to investigate all corners of the camp while Simone started pulling files off shelves. If there were any paper-trail clues to be found she was pretty sure she would find them. She pawed through old equipment catalogs, operating manuals, and a sizeable collection of soft-core porn magazines. Nothing useful there. She turned her attention to the drawers under the workbench and found the usual mix of small tools, broken pencils, and yellowed Scotch tape. A metal box at the end of the bench caught her eye, and here she hit pay dirt: the production records that they would have had to present to their inspector. Under their current state license and a bunch of receipts, she found the barrel production log. Robert had found no fault with their production log, so at least they had the sense to keep track of barrels as they filled them. He had found 113 barrels filled at his inspection date. She turned the sticky pages, noting a reasonably well recorded log of dates and barrel numbers. The last page recorded barrel no. 115, filled the day after Robert's inspection. Certain that the five pages of the log would reveal answers, she laid them out and photographed them carefully. She was putting the contents of the box back as she had found it when an expletive from Serge made her look up.

He was holding aloft a half-liter bottle to which was stuck paper towel bits and cigarette ash. Keeping it at arm's length, he held it out for Simone to decipher the label. *Essence Artificielle Érable*—artificial essence of maple—it read.

"Holy shit. Where the hell did you find that?" Simone was grappling with the possibility that the bottle represented.

"Garbage can," was Serge's simple explanation. "These guys are up to some bad shit."

"I've got their production logs," Simone told him. "Let's get out of here. I need to think about this."

She was reluctant to make a decision about what seemed to be staring them in the face. Her natural caution told her she needed to consider all available information before drawing conclusions. Serge's success with the garbage cans had empowered him, and he was poking into corners around the evaporator. Simone watched as he found a half-empty bottle of organic canola oil, which was the standard de-foamer used by most of the producers, a stash of Jägermeister minis, and, on a small shelf behind the stack, an open sixteen-ounce bottle of caramel food color. He handed her the bottle and she stared at it, searching for understanding. She could think of only one reason why a maple camp would have bottles of fake color and flavor.

"That fucking settles it. I have to report this to Linda. Whatever these assholes did here, there's a serious problem with their syrup. Come on. We need to get to where my phone works. And we need to go find the other end of that road. Maybe we can find out what the hell..." She wasn't ready to admit that she knew what they were looking for, but whatever it was, she needed to find it.

She added photographs of the two incriminating bottles to her evidence record before they reversed the process of getting into the camp, collected the bag of fiddleheads from where they had tucked them in the shade, and made their way back to Serge's camp. They still had time to get through the border and would take both trucks and meet back at the house in Saint-Prosper.

"Bring your records from this year. I need to check yours against theirs again," she called to Serge as he prepared to lock up the camp and she started her truck.

* * *

As soon as Simone drove to within good cell phone reception she pulled over to send a text to Linda, but as she started composing her message she found her conviction that she was onto something fading. All she could report was a mysterious empty sap line and suspiciously over-large production—the last of which MOMP already knew about. She couldn't very well report finding bottles of food additives since that would require revealing illegal breaking and entering, and the extra tubing could have any one of a number of innocent explanations. As for a dead boy and a wounded dog, those were of no concern to MOMP. While it was squarely her responsibility to report anything that might compromise the organic integrity of a product, she had not come across this information in the course of an inspection and was compromised by her obvious bias against the LePages. Once again, she feared sounding like an alarmist fool—or a vendetta-seeking one. She paused to consider her options. It was not her job to find proof, but if she could find enough evidence of foul play to make an accusation stick, she could raise a legitimate concern with MOMP and, even better, prompt some action from the cops.

She put her phone back in her pocket. This was Thursday evening, and nothing much would happen this late in the week at MOMP even if she did send Linda an alert. She had the weekend to find proof that the LePages had somehow cheated on their syrup production and to connect this to their violent acts.

She had a brief word with Steve on her way past his station, claiming urgent need to get back to Ivy, registered at the Canadian post, and drove on to St Prosper.

Ivy, when she found her, was upside down on the sofa, nestled in a pile of plush throws. In this position, her busted jaw and damaged shoulder were at their most comfortable. Mattie was sitting protectively on the other end of the sofa, one long leg between her and the edge. Both boy and dog looked up when Simone entered the house, neither of them moving more that their eyes. Simone dropped her briefcase and laptop, took off her muddy boots, and made her way over to them.

"How's she doing?" she asked.

"She's great," Mattie replied. "She's eating now, and she's been outside. She's about due for another meal."

On cue, Marie-Noëlle produced a child's cereal bowl full of fragrant mush.

"I blended up some chicken breast for her," she said. "That dog food didn't look so good. Her meds are crushed up in it so she needs to eat it all."

Mattie went to roll Ivy up into a sitting position. Her obviously painful shoulder and the contraption on her jaw made repositioning awkward, and she whimpered as she moved, following this with frantic, apologetic tail wagging.

"*Doucement,*" he commanded her, and a look of intense concentration came over Ivy's face. With the air of someone who had developed instant expertise, Mattie placed dollops of the wet chicken mush into the back of her huge, gaping, hardware-filled mouth. The bowl emptied, he fetched a basin, a jug of warm water, and the big irrigating syringe that the vet had supplied and carefully rinsed all food remains from the intricate scaffolding that was holding her jaw together.

"*Voila,*" he said. "I'm doing that every two hours. She likes Mémère's chicken."

"No kidding. You guys are the best. She's going to be fat and spoiled by the time she is healed."

Serge's arrival with the fiddleheads prompted a brief review of the day's discoveries. Mattie's earlier conversational mood vanished at the mention of the LePages and their anomalous tubing. Seeing him retreat into his room, followed by Ivy's anxious regard, Serge pulled Simone into the mud room.

"We'll go find that road on this side of the border," he said quietly. "No need to make a story about it yet."

"Okay. I have to get Ivy to the vet tomorrow afternoon. Gives us time in the morning, right?"

Starting early the next day, they hit the right turn-off onto the old border-crossing road on the first try. The first mile or so was paved road in reasonable shape, passing a small farm and an apparently defunct sugar shack. Where the paving ended, a rough, overgrown track went straight ahead and a dirt road turned left over rising ground. A crooked sign nailed to two trees read *LePage Frères, Construction. Entrée Interdite.*

"Well, that makes sense," Simone said. "They own both sides of the border, kind of. At least, they lease the other side."

From the yard above them, out of sight around the bend in the entrance driveway, they could hear the backup beeping of heavy equipment in operation.

"Let's do this on Sunday," Serge suggested. "They probably don't go to church, but I'll bet they don't work either."

"Deal," agreed Simone, "but let's just see where this old road goes."

Pushing through a short stretch of raspberries and birch for a hundred yards or so, they found themselves looking across a cleared strip directly at the gate they had encountered the day before.

"I'll be damned," Serge said. "That's just too convenient for words. There's something up there that's going to give their game away."

As they made their way back to Serge's truck, two ATVs came full-speed down the paved road from the highway. Simone and Serge ducked into the cover of the woods and watched as they skidded to a halt. Serge let out a hiss as he recognized the two LePage boys. Without getting off their ATVs they sat, gunning their engines, staring at the truck. That the back window sported an *Érablière Thibodeau* logo was painfully evident to both Thibodeaus.

"Shit. We're busted. They'll know it's us," Simone whispered. "We shoulda got out of here while the getting was good."

They waited, fearful of being discovered, but after a brief consultation the two guys turned their machines up the driveway and disappeared in twin spurts of gravel.

"Let's hope they think we are up there," said Serge as they scrambled back to the truck and headed for the safety of Saint-Prosper.

* * *

Getting Ivy to the vet provided useful distraction for the rest of the day. Simone's suggestion that Mattie come with her was met with silent agreement. Serge's big pickup, with room for three in the front, was commandeered and Ivy was loaded carefully onto the seat between them. Her delight at being back at the vet's made Simone smile.

"She's too damn dumb to hate the vet like any normal dog would," she said to Mattie. He rubbed the top of her head affectionately.

"She's a good girl," he said. Ivy, who had mastered the art of face-licking despite her mangled jaw, gave his ear a slurp in agreement.

"You two." Simone laughed. "You make a cute pair."

The vet announced his pleasure at the state of Ivy's repair work. Even in the short time since the attack, healing had made some progress and her wounds showed no sign of infection.

"Good nursing is what it's all about," the understanding man told Mattie when Simone explained that he got the credit for Ivy's care.

They left with instructions to bring her back in two weeks. Her good report called for celebration, and Simone parted with a significant amount of money after Mattie and Ivy had chosen three absurd soft toys from the pet emporium in Saint-Georges. Ivy, carrying her wounded leg and drooling through the metal bracing in her jaw, attracted the attention of everyone in the store. Simone marveled at Mattie's matching pleasure at the fuss, even while he kept his gaze on the dog and never made eye contact with her admirers. If only he had a tail to wag, she thought, it would be so much easier for him.

Simone's impatience at having to wait through Saturday found some relief as she sat down to compare Serge's production logs with the photographs she had made of the LePages' records. Matching dates and production numbers for the two operations, it did not take her long to figure out that the LePages were filling barrels on days when Serge's production slowed or stopped.

"Are they running sap in on their off days?" she speculated to Serge. "Would that even be worth it?"

"There's old family sugar bushes around here," Serge offered. "They might be tapping a few trees and have nowhere to process the sap. Or they may have been shut out of the local market by the Canadian restrictions on production. They could even be buying raw sap, I guess. Maybe we'll get answers up on their site."

"If you need something to do," he added, catching Simone's impatient expression, "go over to LaRivière's and get me spouts and tubing I need. Prices are down right now. I'll give you a shopping list."

The day eventually passed, eased by a soothing shopping spree on Serge's money at the big central supplier of maple equipment. On Sunday morning, right when all good people were in church, they set off once again for the LePage yard. There was no sign or sound of any activity, and feeling the need for the security of the truck, they drove cautiously up the rough drive into the construction yard.

The place was quiet. The drive gave into a large, open gravel-surfaced area that extended to their right toward the border. They paused, engine idling, to take in what they saw. Along the side opposite them, piles of crushed stone, pallets of cement blocks, and other miscellaneous construction materials were lined up in reasonable order. To their left, against dense evergreen woods, was the usual retired shipping container, repurposed as an office and shelter. A generous collection of heavy equipment—some rusting and sprouting young trees, others in apparent working order—occupied the rest of that side of the space. At the farthest end, toward where they supposed they would find the border clearing, an odd assortment of truck beds and smaller equipment was slowly disintegrating.

They checked again to be sure that they were alone. No sign of movement. Serge drove slowly across the open space until they were able to take quick inventory of what appeared to be mostly scrap metal—old truck bodies, dented syrup barrels, wheel hubs, and the inevitable bed springs. Peering behind a large old livestock trailer, Simone spied something more interesting.

"Over here," she said. "This may be what we're looking for."

Working their way around the trailer, they found a surprisingly tidy row of four plastic bulk tanks, sitting on pallets. Each bore a label that, by now, was no real surprise to either Simone or Serge.

"International Sugars, Liquid Sucrose, plus an address in Ontario," Simone read from the label on one tank. The tanks were marked off in liters and gallons, revealing each to hold 2,000 liters, or somewhere around 500 gallons.

"That's it," Serge agreed. "Those sons of bitches are running cheap cane sugar down to their sugar camp. Those absolute bastards. And for that they killed Jean-Yves."

The realization seemed to immobilize him, but Simone wanted to see more. She tugged at his sleeve and made him follow her past the tanks. On the far side, the space was uncluttered save for a narrow thicket of elder and arrowwood and the ubiquitous raspberries. Following a weak path through the brush, they came to the cleared line of the border, which passed a few yards below them. From where they stood, they looked directly down to the gate that was now a familiar sight. There was a faintly flattened path between where they stood and the gate.

"How long was that coil of tubing?" Simone asked. "Would it reach to here?"

"No problem. It's no more than a hundred meters from here. All they have to do is snake that line through the puckerbrush from the other side. Nobody even needs to cross the border."

By mutual silent agreement they headed back to the truck, but as Serge climbed into the driver's seat an idea struck Simone.

"Stay there," she said, and ducked back behind the livestock trailer, her cell phone in her hand.

She set the camera to video, and, taking careful aim, she first photographed the labels on each of the tanks, describing as she did her location and what she was filming. Then she stepped back and stood on the trailer hitch to get a long shot of the line of tanks. To her horror, as she moved the phone across the row of tanks, a figure appeared from somewhere beyond the clutter of old trucks.

Fucking Tommy LePage, her memory told her. She had seen that same face before, that same person, brandishing that same stupid, dangerous weapon. Cold fear hit her like a wave. Her voice vanished and her legs wobbled. She clutched a hitch ring on the side of the trailer as she watched Tommy come toward her, when it dawned on her that he was still too far away to take a shot. The opportunity turned her panic into hot anger. That's the little shit that shot Ivy, she thought, and he can't hurt me yet. Her legs still weren't working right but her voice was back.

"You bastard," she yelled. "What the hell are you doing?"

Tommy liked that question, and had an answer.

"I'm protecting my property," he shouted back. "You're trespassing, just like you were with your dog—and just like your dumb cousin was."

He's been lurking here since Friday, she thought. He knows we are onto him.

"So what if I am? We've figured out what you slime balls have been up to and you're not going to get away with it."

There were only a couple of dead snowplow blades separating her from Tommy now, and she felt her heart stop as he cocked the bow and raised it toward her. Jesus Christ, she thought, I've got no Ivy to protect me this time. She was about to throw herself off the trailer's hitch arm, bracing herself for the impact of the arrow, when he suddenly disappeared. Serge had materialized in his place, holding a hunk of scrap metal and a surprised look on his face.

Simone's legs were now functioning, and she staggered to where Serge was standing over the semiconscious form of Tommy LePage.

"Cold cocked the little sucker," he said. "I heard him coming at you. I don't think he knew I was in the truck. Got him good," he added with satisfaction.

Simone found it necessary to lean against her uncle, who gave her a squeeze before letting her go and reaching down to remove the crossbow from Tommy's slack fingers. The thing had miraculously not fired when he went down. Serge checked the safety but left the little weapon loaded, pointing it at Tommy's lower midsection as he stirred and started to moan.

"Stay back," he ordered Simone. "These things can go off easy." He reached out a careful boot and gave Tommy a poke in the ribs. The boy's eyes opened and he reached for his shoulder where Serge's blow had landed.

Serge was swearing in French, using words that were entirely inappropriate for a Sunday.

"*Debout, charogne,*" he said. "If you ever want to have children, stand up, *sacrement de cochon.*"

They watched with satisfaction as Tommy came to terms with the fix he was in. Simone had been listening for evidence that his brother was with him, but judging from the sheer terror in his eyes and his efforts to comply with Serge's commands, they only had one LePage to deal with.

"I could kill you right here," Serge told was explaining to him. "Just like you killed Jean-Yves, you little piece of shit."

Tommy had evidently watched movies where trapped heroes talk their way out of sticky situations, and fear had loosened his tongue.

"That wasn't my idea," he spluttered as he tried to get his feet under him while not moving his wounded shoulder.

"Bernard was mad. He wanted to scare the kid, not kill him." He thought for a moment and added, "He shouldn't have been going so fast."

The effort to justify the killing of an innocent boy triggered a whole new burst of rage in Serge. He pointed the bow at Tommy's head and moved his thumb toward the safety catch. Tommy went white. Now he was babbling, filling the air with words.

"They shouldn't have been so nosy. None of their business to be snooping around our trees. We weren't hurting anyone—who cares anyway. It's all sugar."

"I freaking care, asshole," Simone said. "I care, because it matters. You don't get to cheat while everyone else is honest. And you sure as hell don't get to kill people and dogs."

Tommy by now was merely whimpering, his verbal torrent reduced to begging Serge not to shoot him. With a snort of disgust, Serge aimed the bow at a spot over his broken shoulder and fired, generating a scream of fear from Tommy. He brought the bow down hard on the nearest snowplow blade and threw it into the pile of parts.

"Get outta here, you miserable little jerk. You won't get away with this. I'll have the police on you, so get the hell out of my sight for now."

Tommy did a three-limbed crawl through the junkyard to where he had stashed a small dirt bike. He got it going and climbed shakily into the seat, and they watched as he wobbled out of the yard.

"What you let him go for?" Simone asked in amazement. The whole encounter had only lasted minutes, but she had been forming pictures in her mind of a trussed-up Tommy in the back of the truck.

"I'm not a cop, and the nearest *Sûreté* station is miles away. He's too scared to do any harm for a while, and besides," he added with a small smile, "you've got it all on video."

He motioned to the phone still in Simone's hand.

"That thing has been running all this time. I could see you videoing before I hit Tommy. We have all the proof we need right there and he doesn't know it. He probably thinks that he can just deny everything. And I'll bet he won't want his big brother to know we beat a confession out of him."

Simone looked at the phone in her hand, which was still recording. She stopped the video and played back the whole scene. Her record of the tanks was clear, and even though the video after that was largely blurry views of her feet, the audio was perfectly clear. All the proof anyone could need, indeed.

"Well, hooray for smart phones," she said, tucking the device carefully into her pocket. "We can play this for the game warden—or the cops, or whoever wants it."

"Yes we can, but not until tomorrow. The border is closed on Sunday. We're done here."

They drove slowly out of the yard and back to the house. Serge needed sleep, but Simone still needed action. She now knew that she could raise the alarm to Linda, who would relay the alert to the big international company that certified The Sugar Shack's organic operation. She went for her laptop as soon as they were back in the house.

Memo to MOMP regarding possible adulteration of organic maple syrup produced by the LePage camp in NW Somerset County,

Maine, she wrote, relishing the reduction of the doubts and fears of the past weeks to a stone cold memo.

As the result of observations made during time spent at my family's business that abuts the LePage camp, I have reason to believe that some or all of the syrup produced by the LePage brothers may be adulterated with nonorganic sugar syrup. I believe that the following barrels (and here she listed the numbered barrels that coincided with the off days of production at Serge's) *are most likely to indicate adulteration. I have photographic evidence that I will be glad to provide.*

She added her name and the date and attached it to an email to Linda. *This is serious. It explains their overproduction. Someone needs to find their syrup and take samples. I'm in Canada right now but I'll be back in Maine asap and can fill you in on details if you need. I wasn't sure about notifying The Sugar Shack. They have picked up already. Trusting you will know what to do.*

With that, she too felt the need for sleep. It's true what they say about coming down from an adrenaline high, she thought. I'm half dead.

* * *

In the following days and weeks, things moved along two approximately parallel tracks. Simone watched with a confusing mix of disgust and relief as established authorities took over her crusade to see the LePage boys face justice.

At MOMP, Linda's efforts to get any response from the LePages to her demands for maps and tap records had largely failed. As the thirty-day deadline for a response to the noncompliance notice approached, Linda sent them the news that she was scheduling a follow-up inspection. This had produced a barely intelligible email that appeared to report the LePage boys' status as "not possible to attend" and offering a different family member instead. Linda's agitation spilled over into a phone call to Simone.

"What the hell do they think we are?" she raged. "They are required to be there—they can't just send in some random third cousin, for chrissake. And I can't send an inspector all the way up there unless I know someone who can deal with these questions will meet them."

Simone could only repeat that it was no surprise that the LePage duo was failing to follow rules. Given the fact that legal matters were also progressing, she assumed they were hiding out as far from the reaches of officialdom as possible. Linda resigned herself to awaiting test results from the LePage syrup.

"That could settle matters," she said. "If their syrup tests positive for adulteration, then this whole records fiasco becomes moot."

Armed with Simone's photos and a detailed written report, she had informed The Sugar Shack organic certifier of the suspected adulteration of the LePage syrup, and for good measure had alerted The Sugar Shack to the problem. This triggered sampling and testing of the suspected syrup, and Simone heard from Linda that results would take a couple of weeks but that, meanwhile, The Sugar Shack had set the whole LePage load aside and was promising to inform MOMP of any results.

On the legal front, things had initially made good progress.

Simone's first instinct, shared with her uncle, had been to get their video to the game warden. He was the only law-enforcement official who had appeared to believe in them, or want to help them. He had seen Jean-Yves lying crumpled in the snow, had been there when Ivy had been shot, and had seen the tree and how the LePages had tampered with it. While Serge did not share Simone's distrust of the authorities, he agreed that the death of one *jarret noir* kid in the backwoods would, on its own, be unlikely to get much attention. Their best hope was that the warden would be able to put his thumb on the scales of justice for them.

Lewey's response to their plea for a meeting had been prompt, and so it was with a sense of hope that they drove back to the camp a mere two days later.

Sitting in the camp, with the obligatory pot of coffee and a boxful of *gallettes* from the one bakery in Saint-Prosper, Simone found it hard to organize and present her trove of new information for Lewey. Suspecting that the young man had limited patience for an outpouring of rage and accusations, Serge took over.

"Here's what we have that's new," he said. "We think we can prove why the LePages wanted to harm our boys. They were cheating on their syrup production and the boys found out—and now we know what they were doing and how they were doing it. And better than that, we got a recorded confession on Simone's phone."

He described the extraneous line of tubing and their discovery of the tanks of cheap syrup. Simone watched as he hesitated and then skipped over any mention of their break-in of the camp. Mention of the food coloring and flavor bottles could wait, but Serge painstakingly explained Simone's analysis of syrup production numbers. The last attempt to lay out this somewhat abstruse data had been interrupted by the chaos of Ivy's shooting.

This time, there being no bloody incidents to distract them, they had Lewey's full attention. He was particularly interested in the line that crossed the border at the old road, and quizzed Serge and Simone on the density of the brush and any signs of use between the two sides of the border.

"You know that old crossing?" Serge asked, quick to notice the warden's interest.

Lewey waved a dismissive hand as if to erase the attention he had drawn to it, but catching a questioning look from Serge he dropped a comment that he was always on the lookout for poachers.

"Eh, true." Serge nodded. "Ever since I was a kid, people have been poaching game here and sneaking it back into Canada."

Well that makes sense, thought Simone. That helps to explain his interest in the LePages. He's probably been watching them for a while. Poaching deer and moose was exactly what you would expect of these two imbeciles. Whatever works, she thought, as long as someone is focused on getting their sorry asses into jail.

"Hey," she said. "No surprise if those two are poaching. Couple of sleazes."

Armed with the new evidence, Lewey promised action. He would take the video, the photographs of the tree and the bogus extra line, and

Simone's calculations, plus his own reports of Ivy's shooting and his inspection of the site to his supervisor and from there it would go to the State Police.

"What good will that do?" Simone asked.

The last time a state trooper had been summoned to the scene, when Ivy was shot, the cop had been unable to see the connection between the injured dog and the snowmobile accident, weeks earlier. He had appeared to regard them as standard byproducts of the basically lawless world of the north woods, and had retreated hastily in his comfortable cruiser.

"Can't avoid them. They have ultimate jurisdiction in a suspicious death. But their criminal division is pretty good," Lewey said with a hint of condescension that Simone noted with approval.

"I'll stay on the case," he assured them. "I have all the evidence. Show me the line you described. I'll get my own pictures of that too."

Simone doubted that anyone would make sense of photographs of a coil of blue tubing, but they dutifully walked Lewey up the length of the line, describing again its discovery and how it connected to the tanks of syrup in the Canadian yard.

The wet spots where they had collected fiddleheads weeks earlier had largely dried out. Patches of boneset were in bloom among the ferns and Simone was impressed when Lewey stopped to rub leaves between his fingers. He offered the bruised leaf to Simone, who caught its faint aroma and bitter taste.

"My grandmother used this," he told her. "Made us kids drink tea she made from it when we ran a fever."

"Some grandma," Simone said. "Mine was the old chicken-soup variety, judging by what my mom gave us."

"I'm Passamaquoddy. Born and raised on Pleasant Point," he said, referencing the Native American tribal lands on the eastern edge of the Maine coast. "My grandmother was old school. Had all kinds of tricks and potions. I like the woods. Bit of a disappointment to my dad. He wanted me to fish with him, but I don't really like the sea. So I figured if I became a game warden I might get work in these woods."

Well, all right, thought Simone. A fellow traveler from a different land. Cool.

Her thoughts were still on medicinal herbs when they reached the end of the tube they had been following, and a soft *"marde"* from Serge brought her back to reality. The coil of blue tubing was gone, cut at the last twist-tie that had secured it to the supporting wire.

"No kidding. Like that's going to make any difference." Simone was disgusted at the pathetic attempt to remove evidence.

"I've got photographs of the whole thing anyway. This just makes them look guiltier—or more stupid," she said.

Lewey had followed the disturbed brush and grasses to the old gate, where a faint trail was still visible across the open cut along the border. He came back to Simone and Serge.

"Looks like they came in just far enough to get that tubing. I guess they didn't want to get too far into Maine. They must know we could be on the lookout for them. They are a lot safer on their side of the border."

There was little else to see, and once back to his truck Lewey took off for Greenville and his headquarters, promising to submit what he had to the authorities and to let the Thibodeaus know if their testimony was needed.

* * *

But that was where all progress on the part of law enforcement came to a frustrating halt.

Simone found herself in limbo, trapped in Saint-Prosper by a combination of Ivy's medical needs and the inertia produced by the lack of any resolution of the case—in her view a strong one—against the LePages.

Ivy was steadily returning to full operating capacity. The two-week return visit to the vet had confirmed that she was healing fast. The hardware in her jaw would have to stay there for another month, and her shoulder injury might leave a lingering gimp, but that just lent character to her already ungainly gait. Mattie's devotion to her care was so evidently therapeutic for him that Simone had not had the heart to take her dog away. Ivy passed her time sleeping on the couch and puttering around the garden with Marie-Noëlle. She and Mattie ventured for short walks into the town, Ivy basking in the attention and Mattie tolerating it on her behalf, and so Simone stayed, glad of an excuse to delay her return to life in Maine, but anxiously waiting for something that would force her to deal with the rest of her life.

She reverted easily to an earlier pattern, helping Serge with line repairs and woods work in the sugar bush. Her communication with Steve, as they crossed through the border, was brief, the guilt she felt at brushing him off only further crimping her ability to talk to him. Her impatience at the slow pace of the law enforcement machine transferred itself to her view of Steve, and she had to work to ignore the voice in her head that told her she was an unfair and judgmental bitch. That Steve had taken time off to help his father with haying, and was not at his post for a full two weeks only added anxiety to her thoughts about him.

Her frustration was mitigated by news from MOMP that the tests done on the LePage syrup had indeed yielded proof of adulteration. With obvious satisfaction, Linda had dispatched the requisite notice of willful noncompliance, informing the LePages that their organic certification had been withdrawn. This action overrode any need to obtain whatever cooperation she had been seeking from LePages. When they failed to take up their option to appeal the finding, as far as Linda was concerned it was all over, and the matter was now out of her hands. Whatever the Department of Agriculture or the Food and Drug Administration chose to do was their problem, and she no longer had to try to squeeze compliance out of sketchy clients.

* * *

On a hot, late July day, Simone, Mattie, and Ivy drove into Saint-Georges. Ivy was greeted at the vet's by her fan club of vet techs and assistants. Her jaw had healed and the hardware set to be removed. Later, with a happy dog now free of the encumbrances of metal bracing, they stopped for celebratory ice creams all around and headed back to Saint-Prosper.

Simone took a deep breath and reached a hand out to Mattie. He withdrew, predictably, so she rested her hand on Ivy's broad backside and tried to find a way to address the fact that Ivy was back to normal and they would have to leave. She had run out of any good reason to stay, and the need to face her future in Maine could no longer be ignored.

149

"She would never have made such a good recovery without you, you know," she said. "We will always owe you."

Mattie was twirling Ivy's ears in his fingers, keeping his gaze on the road ahead, saying nothing.

"I have to get back to Maine and find a job," Simone said, aware that this made little sense to Mattie. She had a job right there, as far as he could tell. Simone tried another tack.

"Serge can only keep me busy for part of the year, and I sort of need to have my own place and my own life."

Obviously this wasn't working either. Mattie had only ever known living with Serge and Marie-Noëlle, and had little or no idea of—or wish to explore—any other option. Simone gave up on explaining an incomprehensible concept, and tackled the subject she had been avoiding.

"Ivy will have to come with me. She's my dog, and even if I wanted her to stay with you, there is no way Serge and Marie-Noëlle would agree. Now that she's all better she needs a lot of work, and room. She's too big and bouncy."

Mattie was silent, but his face showed a flash of the fear and anxiety that had been so evident weeks ago. It had retreated lately, though he was a long way from the kid he had been before all this started.

"You'll be fine," Simone offered weakly. "Marie-Noëlle needs your help at the library and you could maybe get a job at the shelter, or at a vet's. You are super good with animals. They love you."

Mattie's sad expression did little to reassure her that she had offered anything useful. She knew that Ivy's recuperation had been a big deal for Mattie, tapping a seam of innate fellow feeling for a hurt being, but leaving Ivy with him had never been an option—not for her, not for Marie-Noëlle, and not for the dog. The Thibodeaus were not pet owners. Animals, for them, meant farm work, and she had never known them to have, or want, a house pet.

They reached Saint-Prosper to find Serge in an animated state. Word of the LePages had traveled on the local grapevine. Uncle Benoit was telling his cronies that his nephews had dodged the American legal system, and that as long as they stayed out of the US they were at little risk. Serge was seething, and Marie-Noëlle's usual calm was proportionately ruffled.

Lewey had reported a successful transfer of evidence to the State Police, and that the case had progressed to a grand jury, who had returned an indictment of manslaughter. An arrest warrant now existed in Maine, but that seemed to be where everything stopped. Any effort toward extradition and resolution was evidently dead, and the LePages were celebrating.

"Well, shit," Simone exploded. "Manslaughter, my ass. They killed Jean-Yves and, 'Oops, sorry, we didn't mean it' is a defense now? *Câlice,*" she swore, getting a look from Serge that was part reprimand and part approval that she was now cursing like a true *Beauceron.*

"Later," he said to her. "We'll talk." His glance toward Mattie had the desired effect, and Simone took her frustration out for a quick evening walk with Ivy.

Once Mattie was safely in bed, the three of them sat around the kitchen table.

"How dare that fat cat Benoit brag that they are getting away with what they did?" Serge asked. "They have destroyed a family and scared my grandson half to death. And they've given the organic syrup business a bad name." He caught Simone's eye and added, "They scared you and hurt Ivy too. I'm sorry…"

Marie-Noëlle had been thinking.

"I don't hate easily," she admitted, "but those *petits salauds* don't deserve an easy life after the harm they have done."

"There is a perfectly good arrest warrant out for them in Maine," Serge pointed out. "If we could only…"

"They would never cross the border for us, and if they tried, the Immigration guys would get them," Simone said.

Marie-Noëlle had another problem on her mind, and turned the conversation to Mattie. He wasn't doing well, she said. She sensed his enduring fear of leaving the house, and knew that he dreaded the presence of the two LePages. He only ventured out if Ivy was with him. She gives him courage, she said. She looked at Simone.

"I know you have to take her, and she can't stay here, but he is afraid of those two boys. They know he blew the whistle on them. As long as they are at liberty he will be frightened of what they could do to him."

Simone could feel the impatience and anger that had been brewing in her for weeks come rushing to the front of her consciousness. She needed to do something, anything. She hadn't come this far to see those two jerks skate out of trouble, protected by a slow-moving, cross-border legal system that put a remote manslaughter problem—that might only have been an accident—on its back burner. One dead French boy was too easy for them to ignore, but they didn't know Mattie, or how badly he needed to know that the threat these fools posed was resolved. They hadn't carried a terrified dog out of the woods or faced a weapon aimed right at them, twice. (Well, true, she remembered, Serge had shot past Tommy's ear and scared the little shit to hell. That had been nice.) Unable to stay still, she got up roamed around the house. Finding no outlet for her energy, she grabbed a plateful of jam-filled cookies from the counter and sat back down at the table.

Serge had been working on a thought, and addressed a seemingly random question to the space above the cookie plate.

"What will happen to their lease?" he asked.

"Huh?" Simone steered her thoughts back from fantasies about kidnap and car accidents to Serge's question.

With arrest warrants against them in the US, and their organic certification withdrawn, it was clear that the LePages were abandoning all plans to continue operating their camp.

"I guess it's available. And a new owner could get certified no problem. It was the finished syrup, not the woods or the process, that they fucked up. Why do you ask?"

"Well, if a new leaseholder was interested, would he need to meet them there?" he wondered.

Simone thought she could see where he was going, but it didn't offer much help.

"Not really," she said. "A lawyer or Uncle Benoit would do. And it wouldn't have to be at the camp, anyway, I don't think."

Serge was still working on an idea.

"What if someone said they needed to see the camp—equipment, records—stuff they would want to learn from the operators?"

Simone let that scenario play in her mind.

"I dunno. They would still have to cross the border and risk getting nabbed there. You're not suggesting they would come over to talk to you, are you?"

That idea seemed to be full of holes, but Serge was ahead of her.

"No. They wouldn't trust me. And besides, they know I know their place too well to need a guided tour."

He was quiet long enough for both of them to arrive at the same point together.

"Pierre," they said in unison.

"Nobody would ever suspect a Bolduc of something underhanded," Serge said, "and they don't know that Pierre was there when they shot Ivy. They may think he doesn't know the trouble they are in."

"If anyone could fool them, Pierre and the rest of those Bolducs probably could," Simone had to admit. They had a lot of standing in the maple sugar world of the Maine producers, and the LePage dopes might be flattered enough by their attention to risk a trip in to their camp.

They sat silent for a while, but before the evening was much older, a plan had started to take shape.

* * *

And now here she was, on a hot, buggy late summer day, perched uncomfortably on a bench in Serge's sugar house with the game warden on an old chair beside her, both taking care to keep themselves out of view of anyone looking through a window.

Outside, concealed at least partially behind the camp, two state troopers sat in their cruisers, and inside the camp, Serge and the game warden's sergeant kept their heads down. The attempts to stay out of sight were spurious, in Simone's view. The action was all going to be over at LePages', and there was no way to see into Serge's camp from there. It felt to her as if the idea of a sting had infected all these guys with an old-fashioned desire to act out their childhood fantasies of cops and robbers. Still, some discretion was in order. It was just as well not to advertise their presence, even at the height of summer when the sugar camps were largely empty.

The party had assembled before dawn in the spacious yard at the nearest of the two Bolduc camps. Why four guys needed four separate vehicles, Simone could not comprehend. You people ever heard of carpooling? she wanted to ask, but the two state troopers did not look like the ridesharing kind, and Lewey and the game warden sergeant had come in from different starting points. Oh, well, she figured. At least they are here and looking reasonably awake. They had important work to do.

Setting up this scenario had taken some weeks of planning, but Simone's determination to bring about a resolution had powered them through. It started with a pie-fueled meeting at the Bolduc family home on the outskirts of Saint-Georges. Pierre and his cousin Marc, the family member responsible for the second Bolduc camp, had listened to Simone's pleas for revenge and to Serge's reasoned argument that they just had to find a way to get the LePage guys back into Maine. Two weeks and another pie later, they sat around the same table and reviewed progress.

The Bolduc cousins had needed little persuading. Their view of the world easily embraced lending their shoulders to help turn the wheels of justice. Marc, as a senior member of the family and at a remove, geographically and personally, from the original crime, had approached Benoit LePage, professing interest in acquiring the lease, and the camp, from his nephews. Informed that he had rid himself of any ties to the maple business, but promising to get his nephews to show up, Benoit had arranged a meeting.

"You were right about flattery working," Marc reported. "They fell right for the idea that we would value their business."

"Nice," Simone said, "but how did you get them to agree to meet you at the camp?"

"Not so easy. Needed a lot more *foutaise* on our part," Marc said, with Pierre nodding agreement.

"They liked the idea that we wanted them to show us their operation and their trees in detail. We acted like we needed their advice on how it all worked."

Marc's indefinably French interaction between his eyebrows and his shoulders told Simone how much they had enjoyed hoodwinking two creeps.

"We had to work a little harder on just how to make it all happen," Pierre continued. "They are smart enough to know that going through the border was going to be a bad idea."

Marc's hands had joined his shoulders in expressing his amusement.

"We told them we knew they had that yard just over the border and we were certain that they could outsmart the border patrol and get across without being caught. That family has been doing that for years, *après tout*," said Pierre.

"I even offered to meet them on the Maine side with the ATV," said Marc. "And it didn't hurt that we threw around some quite unreasonably high numbers for the value of their lousy facility."

"We told them they both had to come so they could both sign agreements, but I don't think they trust each other enough to do anything without looking over each other's shoulders. So that was it. We have a plan. They are going to sneak across before dawn, one of us will meet them and get them into their camp, and the rest is up to you."

Date and time were agreed on, and Simone was deputized to contact warden Lewey and let him know that she hoped and expected that someone would be there to arrest the two goons. The Bolducs had promised to bring volumes of paperwork, planning to make the process last while they documented every piece of equipment and reviewed years of past production records. This would give whatever cops and wardens were there time to emerge from hiding and haul the LePages into custody. That was the plan, anyway.

Now they were in position. Notified that the LePages would be in Maine, the four officers of the law had made their way to the camps. The Bolducs had left for the LePage camp, Marc on the big, tracked ATV that got them around the woods under any conditions, and Pierre on his dirt bike, his excuse being that they would leave room in the LePage yard for police vehicles, though Simone knew that he would take any chance to zoom around on the bike. As Simone understood it, Pierre would stay at the LePage camp while Marc would meet the LePages before it got light. Pierre would radio progress to Lewey, who would in turn signal the cops, using the state-issued short-wave system they all carried.

With nothing to do but sit and wait for a signal from the Bolducs, Simone felt the need to make conversation. Lewey had been consistently helpful from the beginning, and she wanted him to feel that even if the plan failed, his day had not been entirely wasted.

"How often do you get stuff like this?" she asked.

"Deliberate criminality?" Leonard Lewey replied. "Very little, really. There are always poachers up in these woods, and plenty of petty stuff. People running too many traps, hunting after sundown, that sort of thing. And risking their lives speeding. They think no one is watching them on these woods roads."

He paused, remembering an incident that had amused him.

"Couple of years back I helped a guy find his ATV. Someone took it out of his camp yard and I found it buried in the woods way off the road. Told the owner and he and his girlfriend hiked in and drove it home. Wish we had set up a trail cam to record the fellow when he found the toy he had stolen had been stolen back!"

"Did you catch the ATV thief?" Simone asked.

"No. Never heard a word around the camps as to who it could have been."

"Well," Simone said, "let's hope we get the bad guys this time."

They sat in silence for a while, Lewey staring at the little two-way radio he had brought with him. The other half of the system was in Pierre Bolduc's pocket, either in or near the LePage camp.

* * *

Since dawn had broken there had been no signal from Pierre. He had let them know that Marc had gone to retrieve the LePages, but since then the radio had gone silent. Caution obviously prevailing, Simone concluded. It might take them a while to get the boys into a situation where arrests could be made.

The tension was killing Simone. The Bolducs had planned to lull the LePages into taking them seriously by suggesting an inspection of trees and sap lines on the way back to camp. The idea amused Simone. How were two of the best syrup makers in the area going to pull off a convincing pretense that the LePage setup was anything but shoddy? she wondered. She had to trust the Bolducs, and remember how devastated Pierre had been when Serge had explained how Jean-Yves's death had been engineered.

Her racing heart was making her nervous—and chatty.

"So how did you get to be a game warden?" she asked Leonard, finding the silence intolerable. He was a man of few words, but he seemed glad to share his story with a sympathetic listener.

"The tribe owns land up here—beautiful, untouched maple woods," he told her. "We've got a syrup business here and I used to come up and help when it was getting started."

That apparently exhausted his conversational capacity, but the silence had become more companionable. Simone prompted him for details on his career choice.

"I was a good kid in school," he said, "on the football team, decent grades, that stuff. And I've had this thing with the woods forever, so game warden looked like a good idea. Soon as I could I did the trainings—bit of a gut-buster but I made it through. My dad wasn't thrilled to start with. Like I told you, I was supposed to want to go fishing with him."

She offered an "I know how you feel. My dad feels let down by me, and I love these woods too," before they resumed their focus on the radio that Leonard held at the ready, waiting for Pierre's signal.

Serge emerged from the camp where he had been sitting with Lewey's sergeant. Inactivity was making him restless. As he approached them, the radio burped a couple of times and they heard Pierre's voice, muffled but recognizable.

"They're here. Coming into the camp. Give us ten minutes to get them talking. The front door is open."

* * *

What followed stayed with Simone as one of the best moments of her life.

The state troopers had made it clear that civilian interference in this project was not needed. They had delivered threats about safety and their responsibilities in a manner that Simone found insulting, given that she and Serge had set this whole thing up and, if not for them, the cops wouldn't be here at all, ready to make nice arrests for their record books.

And not even a "thank you," she thought. Nonetheless, following their orders, she and Serge hung back while the troopers' two huge SUVs, followed by the wardens in Lewey's truck, took off for the LePage camp.

Watching the cavalcade disappear out of his drive was too much for Serge. He had already decided that there was no way they were going to miss out on watching the LePage boys meet their fate. His ATV keys were in his pocket, and Simone was right behind him, as he headed out of the camp to the waiting vehicle. As they left the Thibodeau drive and started down the short stretch of road to the LePage camp, a dirt bike at full, screeching engine speed spun off the road and, wobbling as the rear wheel churned in the loose dirt, wove its way past them and up Serge's drive.

"Go, go, go," Simone yelled at Serge as he took in what was happening. "That's fucking Bernard, for chrissake. "GO! Follow him."

The bike was Pierre Bolduc's. It was a beast, she knew, a racing stunt-riders' dream, and Bernard LePage seemed to be having some difficulty controlling the thing.

With Simone pounding on the seat between them as if goading a horse, Serge swung the ATV back the way they had come. Bernard and the bike were out of view. They could hear him heading up the one road out of the camp, up toward the pump house.

"Don't let him get away," Simone shouted. The ATV was no match for the powerful bike, but pursuit had to be tried. They knew that trails led from Serge's road down to the old powerline road and the border, and given some luck, Bernard would be able to reach the crossing and be back in Canada before they could stop him.

The ATV, built for function rather than speed, had just turned onto the pump house road when Simone realized that they could no longer hear the bike. Serge was focused solely on getting as much speed out of the four-wheeler as he could, and it was Simone who was about to shout a question when they rounded the corner at the top of the trail. Her question was cut off in midair. There in front of them was a scene that brought a jolting flash of recognition into Simone's mind. The bike lay across the path, and the figure of a boy sprawled across the trail.

"Oh, shit, no." Whoever it was, Simone could not face another dead body. She froze to her seat, but Serge was up and had reached the unmoving form of Bernard, sprawled face down in the moss. She watched as he bent over the boy and abruptly straightened out and pushed the toe of his boot into the body's mid-section.

"ROPE!" he shouted. "In the box."

Simone recovered her ability to move. This one wasn't dead, and he needed securing. Grabbing a hank of all-purpose line from the toolbox on the back of the ATV, she stumbled to where Serge was staring down at the still more or less motionless Bernard. He had turned a face, white with fear and marred by a good-sized gash across its forehead, to his captors. He looked dazed, but his understanding of the situation was developing.

"Got you, you little *trou de cul*," Serge said. He took the rope from Simone and, with the expertise of someone with a lifetime of jury-rigging repairs around a farm and a camp, lashed Bernard's hands together behind his back and added a few turns to bind his arms to his body for good measure. The kid's yelp of pain did nothing to stop Serge's trussing project.

At that moment, the grinding of another engine became apparent, and the Bolducs' tracked machine, with Pierre and Lewey up, came around the corner.

"What the hell happened here?" Pierre asked as Lewey, business as usual, inspected Serge's tie-down job.

Simone had not taken in how the bike, and Bernard, had come to grief, but now she could see that the rear wheel was entangled in the very same wire that had killed Jean-Yves. Her mind flicked back over the summer's activities. Sure enough, she knew, no one had fixed that wire. Warned by police to leave the site as it was until all need for evidence was met, they had let it lie, glad to have an excuse to avoid the place. It looked as if the front wheel had kicked the wire up and into the rear wheel, and Bernard had been pitched over handlebars, his face meeting the trunk of the very tree that he had tampered with. It was too perfect. The revenge of the woods. Standing there, Simone realized that all anxiety and tension had left her. The action and the outcome had produced a sense of calm that, even now, she could feel.

Lewey was still examining Bernard, asking questions about his fingers and toes, apparently worrying about neck injuries. A tedious, and to Simone's mind unnecessary, assessment was carried out to ensure that he could be righted to his feet and transported back down the hill. Who cares, she thought. Paralysis would be a fine result. Jean-Yves hadn't had that option. But she dutifully waited, noting as she did that Pierre was paying more attention to his bike than to Bernard, solicitously righting it and untangling the wire from its wheel.

The field check of Bernard's injuries apparently satisfied Lewey that moving him was safe. With Pierre on one side and Lewey on the other, Bernard was frog marched, stumbling and moaning, to the ATV, ready for the ride back to the camps. Serge and Simone went ahead, both eager to know what had become of Tommy, now that his brother's downfall was certain.

The scene in the LePage camp was right out of a B movie, and Simone was guiltily aware that she was enjoying it. A trembling, handcuffed Tommy LePage was balanced on a stool, dwarfed by the two enormous state policemen. One was on his radio, getting the news from the game wardens that brother Bernard was in custody and that the warden was bringing his catch in. In the morning light now edging in through the open door, Simone could see the look of complete defeat on Tommy's face. He was never cut out to be a criminal, she thought. Just too dumb and scared to figure out a better way to make his life work.

She left the quaking kid to his captors, and found Marc and the game warden sergeant in the yard, listening for the arrival of the ATV. When it came into sight, with Bernard LePage squeezed between Pierre and Lewey, a look of pain and confusion on his face, Simone knew that a chapter was closing. This is why we have these guys, she thought, watching as the cops loaded a LePage into each of their cruisers. All the mumbo-jumbo, announcing their arrest and their rights, had played over her head. She found that she didn't care. They were, indeed, in custody, and likely to remain there for a while. They were poster boys for flight risk, and unlikely to get more than a court-appointed lawyer, so they were off the streets and out of the Thibodeaus' lives for a good, long, threat-free while.

* * *

Exhaustion beat out elation as Simone and Serge rolled slowly into the driveway in Saint-Prosper. Simone barely felt the need to celebrate. Evil, or some weak but nasty version of it, had, for now, been vanquished and all she wanted to do was to sleep. The drive back to Saint-Prosper had started out with a sense of marvel. It was done. Those two toxic sources of anxiety and fear were gone, one to county jail and one—for now—to the hospital. Whatever became of them, their power to harm had been neutralized. The desire to move on, to put all that behind her, was now stronger than any thoughts of the past.

Mattie and Ivy were in their customary formation on the sofa. Ivy, no longer willing to pass whole days sleeping, zoomed around the house in ecstatic reception mode, skidding on the parquet floor and popping wheelies on the carpet. Her ability to sense a need for quiet companionship was apparently only activated by Mattie, and it took a while for Simone to calm her down and return her to her sofa buddy.

Mattie looked at his knees and waited. He had known what Serge and Simone's mission had been when they set out the day before. Simone pushed Ivy off the sofa and dropped into the empty corner. Rather than disturb Mattie with physical touch, she stretched her arm along the back of the sofa toward him, reaching out but keeping her distance.

"We got them, Matts," she said. "They're gone. Done. Both hauled off by Maine policemen. They won't be bothering any of us again."

Mattie's eyes met hers in uncharacteristic contact. *Really?* they asked.

"It's true, babe," she assured him. She wanted to promise him that they would never be back, but he knew the life of Saint-Prosper as well as she did. He understood that the chances of two disgraced boys ever making it in this town after the humiliation of their arrest in the US was slim to none, even if the legal system in Maine failed to put them away for as long as they deserved.

"I'll give you the details in the morning," she told Mattie, "but now I need a shower and bed."

She doubted that he would want to know any more. He would build a wall against the memories of the months since Jean-Yves had died, and find his own way to move on, freed, she hoped, of immediate fear.

* * *

The next day, Simone was confronting her own need to retrieve a life that was not bounded by the LePages. The greenhouse in LaGrange had lost what little appeal it ever held. That's not me, she could hear herself say. Flowers and gardens are all very well for the home-based types, but I want the woods and a canoe—and a place of my own. How the fuck do I get that? she asked herself.

Start with a real job, came the voice. *Criss,* I sound like my mother, she thought. Perhaps I should go hang with her for a while and figure this stuff out.

Mattie was on her mind as she packed her truck. He emerged from his room and watched as she gathered Ivy's bed and toys. With a solemn and ceremonial gesture, he handed Simone her leash. He didn't say a word, but managed to look Simone directly in the eyes and, miraculously, reach a tentative hand toward her. She fist-bumped him and took the leash.

"You are the strongest person I know," she told her cousin, risking a grab for him before he escaped.

He met her hug with little resistance and she laughed.

"Go get 'em, tiger," she told him. "You are going to be great. And don't forget. Ivy and I will love you forever."

She was delighted to see a smile and a rich blush on Mattie's face. He is in there, she knew, a great and sensitive person who would find a way out of his cage of anxiety.

Leaving Serge and Marie-Noëlle was hard. For almost six months they had fought together to keep evil at bay. Jean-Yves was never coming back, but so much had been won. They were not given to effuse expression, and the ties among them were well understood, so comforting familiarities about taking care and keeping in touch were exchanged and Simone packed Ivy into her truck and set out for the border.

She had business to do there, and was unsure how to accomplish it. She was acutely aware that she had ground to make up. Steve had remained friendly throughout the summer, but she couldn't escape the thought that she had done some damage by blowing him off for so many weeks. She was profoundly confused and unwilling to address the source of her distress. What did she want? Problem was, she didn't know. You don't need a boyfriend, can't be bothered, the inner harridan told her, but that did not seem to be the issue here. She decided to focus on the immediate and the obvious. This was a nice guy who had given her the perfect dog and had never crossed a line of her defenses. She owed him friendship and a whole lot of thanks. The boyfriend thing could await further information.

He was busy with a line of logging trucks when she pulled into the station. Ivy caused a commotion by charging the office in search of one of her many best friends, and Simone had to pull her out, apologizing to the drivers, unable to explain why the border agent was being attacked by an enthusiastic pit bull.

"Stay in the truck. You are an embarrassment to the whole world," she told the chagrined dog. With the truckers on their way, she found Steve in a businesslike mood and apologized again for Ivy's lack of boundaries.

"She needs a whole lot of exercise," was her explanation. "I am going to spend some time with my Mom. Ivy thought maybe you would come for a hike with us."

She hoped fervently that Steve would understand that this was an admission that she had been unable to deal with anything but the LePages for weeks, but that was over now and she was attempting catch-up. It seemed like a lot to convey through one puny invitation, but it was the best she could do.

She got a raised eyebrow from Steve and a small smile.

"A hike would be good," he replied, to her infinite relief. "I am booked in with my pops next week to help him get hay into the barn. He got a good late second cut."

"Oh, great. Good. I mean, Ivy will be pleased. Me too," Simone's ability to form sentences had deserted her again, but she managed to secure a promise from Steve that he would call when he got to Albion.

"See you. Thanks," she managed, and retreated to Ivy and the truck.

As they set out yet one more time for the ride down the Golden Road, Ivy positioned herself against the passenger side door, hanging her head out of the window and occasionally barking at whatever caught her attention.

"Sorry, hellhound," Simone told her. "You can't do that. It's obnoxious behavior, especially in an ugly brute like you. You've been spoiled rotten on a couch for too long. You need to get some real exercise."

She had anticipated the need, and when a long, quiet stretch of the road presented itself, she got Ivy out of the car and rigged up a training device—a long pole with a slip leash attached to one end. She jammed the other end into loops of line—purloined from Serge from the same hank that had been used to tie up Bernard LePage—attached to her seat back, and stuck Ivy's head through the leash, securing the dog in reasonable safety a few feet from the truck. Ivy looked confused but willing to learn, as Simone slipped the truck into gear and started down the road at a slow crawl. She hoped she wouldn't strangle the dog before she learned the new trick, but at least she couldn't get under the wheels. Encouraged by a combination of threats and praise from Simone, Ivy soon had it figured out, and trotted beside the truck obligingly. She would have the redneck running thing down with a little more practice, Simone concluded.

"You're a good girl," she told Ivy. "We'll soon have you fighting fit. Then we can sic you on those morons at the Moose Crossing."

They stopped where a culvert carried a small stream under the road. Released from the trainer device, Ivy flopped into the brook, flattening herself out for maximum contact with the cool water. Simone sat watching her, catching the unchecked delight coming from the dog.

"Whoever wrote 'Don't worry, be happy' must have known you in another life," she told Ivy, settling the wet and contented dog onto an old towel on her seat. Ivy experimented with a new move, rolling sideways as if to arrive on Simone's lap by accident.

"Don't even try it," Simone said, flapping at her with a dirty glove. "You are wet and smelly and I don't love you."

Ivy sighed and curled up on her own seat, shooting Simone a reproachful look that said *Have it your way, but you can't blame a girl for trying.*

Cruising slowly east down the familiar road, Simone felt the tensions of the past months fading. She hadn't asked for that job, but she had seen it through, and now she knew she could move on. An idea had been growing slowly in her mind and she was eager to find peace and quiet and a good internet connection where she could follow it up with some research.

Summer days before school started meant plenty of traffic on the Golden Road. Families who could brave the blackflies and distance from comfortable amenities found their way up into the woods and lakes, looking for fishing holes and camp sites. Spotting a moose in an alder swamp along the north shore of Seboomook lake, Simone pulled the truck over and sat and watched a cow and her calf, half asleep in the hot afternoon, twitching their long ears and occasionally searching the shallow water for a snack. Global warming was threatening the moose herd with a plague of ticks, unknown in Maine until longer, warmer summers had brought the infestation north. It was too early for the winter parasites to be on the moose, and these two looked plump and happy, but Simone knew that the calf had about a fifty percent chance of surviving the winter as tens of thousands of ticks would drain its blood and its life. Fucking climate change and the powers-that-be who had ignored decades of warnings, she thought. Maine will lose the maple business if the seasons change enough, she knew. Sugar bushes farther south were already feeling the pinch as the critical sap-flow weeks became too short for them to make money. She watched the serene moose with a feeling of sadness.

Warned that disturbing resting wildlife was not her job, Ivy sat placidly and watched with Simone.

"We'll come back up here and spend some real time," Simone promised her. "I'll show you all kinds of neat stuff."

Past Ripogenus Dam, where the Penobscot River offers the best rafting run in the state, the pressure of too many people prompted Simone to close the windows and head straight for Liberty.

* * *

She knew she could face her mother now. She no longer felt the need to make excuses for how she had spent her summer. Despite the small rock that was lodged in her gut that said she had triggered events leading to Jean-Yves's death, she knew that she and Ivy and Serge had done a good thing. Those cheaters had to be stopped, and when they turned into murderers, they had to be caught, if only for Mattie's sake. I don't have to defend myself against charges of wasting my life, she told herself. And besides, she had a plan.

The house in Liberty was quiet when she arrived. A note on the kitchen table under a bottle of good red wine announced that Ellie was sailing for two or three days, and suggested that Simone could make herself useful by picking beans from the garden. There was instruction on chicken care and the news that firewood was to be delivered and she could start stacking it "if she needed a job."

I get it, Simone thought. No such thing as a free bed. No problem. She was happier when she had a job to do.

But first things first. She had invited Steve to hike with her. The plan had been confirmed through one phone call. Now she had some serious preparation to do.

An upside to all that time spent in Saint-Prosper and the camps: she hadn't spent much money. Serge had pressed a wad of folded green bills into her hand as she left, insisting that she take it, and she still had some of her spring greenhouse earnings. With a pocketful of cash and an idea, she drove to the fancy new gourmet foods place on Route 1 in Rockport, ground zero of the wealthy summer yachting scene.

Stick to the classics, she told herself, collecting a cute wicker shopping basket from the front counter. After a childhood with Ellie, whose early life had been one of privilege in what she called "the Home Counties" of southern England, Simone knew her way around this stuff. She was hoping to impress without seeming to show off. Forget the cans of *foie gras* and the weird liqueur made from spruce buds. She located a fresh baguette, sweet cream butter, and some newly sliced prosciutto. Good start, she thought. Who doesn't love the best ham sandwich in the world? It being harvest season in Maine, huge, pinkish tomatoes, cat-faced and discolored on their shoulders, were an obvious addition, joined in her basket by a wet lump of fresh mozzarella, safe in a plastic container, and a fat bunch of basil. Okay, getting there. She added two locally brewed lagers and two IPAs, passing over the array of proseccos as too pretentious. Enormous green olives caught her eye, and two fruit tarts, with shiny glazed strawberries sitting on custard in a crisp pastry nest, begged her to take them too. Fearful that she didn't have enough to make a hike last all day, she picked a durable-looking cheese and a second baguette, plus a baggie full of home-made dog treats for Ivy. Hard-boiled eggs from Ellie's hens would round out the meal.

Damn, she thought as she watched her extravagance translate into a dollar figure. This shit is expensive. She reminded herself that she owed Steve at least that much, and handed over most of the cash she had come with. Please, God, she prayed, don't let him be a white bread and American cheese kind of guy. That would make this a really stupid idea.

She had studied the maps of the forty-seven mile Hills to the Sea trail that stretches from inland Unity to Belfast on the coast. Maps suggested that it passed through the Frye Mountain State Game Management Area, which offered "scenic views" and various ecosystems to walk through. That should work, she figured.

Starting earlier than was necessary, Simone took down a pack basket from a shelf in Ellie's mud room. It was a beautiful thing, made by a Penobscot Indian basket maker in Old Town from brown ash splints. She lined it with an old quilt, packed her food purchases carefully, and added cold packs. Cruising Ellie's bookshelves, she found a skinny paperback of Wendell Berry poems and a battered copy of T. S. Elliot's *Old Possum's Book of Practical Cats*. Nice balance, she thought. She tucked both books between the quilt and the basket. If bringing poetry to a picnic seemed too cheesy, or the moment wasn't right, they could stay there and no one need ever know.

At the appointed time, Steve, in Carhartts and a T-shirt, more farm boy than officer of the law, showed up and survived Ivy's greeting. He had never been to the Frye Mountain preserve, and announced he was ready to hike until Ivy was exhausted or the day ended, whichever came first.

For the first hour, they walked with little conversation. Bless the man for not needing to chat, Simone thought. The trail started out along a stream and crossed abandoned farm fields, now invaded by patches of brush and tree growth but still home to astonishingly colorful arrays of early blue asters, golden rod, and black-eyed Susans.

"I don't know why people think they can do better than this," she told Steve. "They spend all kinds of money on exotic flowers that can never be more beautiful than a meadow in Maine at the end of summer."

Her appreciation of the wildflowers was shared by a population of bumblebees, working the flowers with complete disregard for Ivy's interest in them. Steve grabbed her collar, pointing her up toward Frye Mountain.

Reaching higher ground and a view south over farms and woodland, they found a flat rock and Simone unpacked her picnic. She spread expensive treats on the quilt and commanded Ivy to stay the hell away from them. Steve's reaction was swift.

"Oh, heaven," was his greeting to the baguette and prosciutto sandwich. "I spent time in Germany in the army, and a buddy and I used to go looking for good food. I haven't had a sandwich like this since then."

They ate in silence, until Simone decided to risk an unburdening.

"I'm sorry I was so—I mean, I feel like I was ignoring you, and you've been…" This wasn't the eloquence she had been hoping for, but Steve seemed to get it.

"No worries," he said. "I'm happy to wait. You've had a lot on your plate. And I'm glad we are here."

"Me too. Thanks." That pretty much covered it, Simone thought. No need to say more.

Steve was examining the basket, and to her embarrassment had found the books of poetry.

"Berry," he said. "Good stuff." He picked up the little book, which fell open at a well-used page.

"Peace of Wild Things," he read.

When despair for the world grows in me
and I wake in the night at the least sound
in fear of what my life and my children's lives may be,
I go and lie down where the wood drake
rests in his beauty on the water, and the great heron feeds.
I come into the peace of wild things
who do not tax their lives with forethought

of grief. I come into the presence of still water.
And I feel above me the day-blind stars
waiting with their light. For a time
I rest in the grace of the world, and am free.

"I kept that one in a pocket when I was in Iraq," he said. "I always knew I would get back to Maine and the wilderness."

Wow, thought Simone. Not just any old farm boy. Another "me too" would sound redundant, so she sat in silence. The musky smell of the woods in late summer and the tapping of a woodpecker on a nearby snag was better than a lot of talk.

"Hairy," Steve said quietly. It took Simone a moment to realize that he was identifying the woodpecker, and she laughed.

"Thought you meant the cheese," she said. Unwrapped, the chunk of sheep-milk cheese had whiskers on it that she had not planned for. They fed the rind to Ivy and made sandwiches for the walk back to the truck.

The beer, and the shared lunch break, loosened Simone's tongue. She had ideas she wanted to try out on someone.

"I've been thinking about Game Warden school," she said. "I googled it. There are training programs, but it looks doable."

Steve took a while to think about this.

"You would be a great game warden," was his response, "and it's about time they got some women on the force."

"I liked the guy that helped us get those assholes," Simone went on. "Seems like the wardens are the go-to guys in the woods. If you want something done, you need them." She didn't want to disparage other branches of law enforcement. They all had their place, but the woods were the wardens' domain, and the other outfits seemed to respect that.

"They are a pretty independent bunch," Steve said. "Ornery at times." He seemed to have personal experience, but added with a chuckle, "You would fit right in."

Well, thought Simone, I guess that means I don't have to apologize to him for being a pain in the ass. That saves a lot of trouble and time.

"Gee, thanks." She returned his chuckle. "You know, it was weird but I just loved catching those bad guys. It was a rush. Felt so great."

Memories of that day came flooding back. She hadn't fully down-loaded and examined all that had happened, but now she recounted the day to Steve, explaining her feelings of triumph as the two LePages were taken away, stripped of their power to menace and cheat. She had to admit that she had been mostly a bystander, and that a desire to be an active enforcer of the laws of the woods had been growing in her ever since. She described the scene at the LePage camp: the two cops, their uniforms clean and creases intact, and the muddy action figure of Leonard Lewey four-wheeling the captive out of the woods. She wanted that life.

"You should definitely go for it," he said. "They would be lucky to have you."

They lapsed back into silence, the day now providing a sense that shared space and time had brought them together.

The sun was going down when they got back to the cottage in Liberty. Simone had been wondering about the bottle of wine and whether she wanted to ask Steve to stay and share it with her. There were sausages in the fridge, and green beans to burn, and she was reluctant for the day to end. Any such thoughts were interrupted by the sight of a familiar blue Honda in Ellie's yard.

"Oh shit. Jocelyne? Really? What the heck is that about?" She was still reacting to the unexpected when two figures emerged from the house.

"Fuck. It's my dad. And his girlfriend," she started to explain, stopping herself when she remembered that Steve, of course, knew who they were. How many times had he checked their passports, she wondered?

"What in God's name can they be doing here?" she asked.

Her surprise was sharpened by the knowledge that she had neglected to maintain regular contact with Gilles. He was another victim of the summer's stress, she knew, but still, she felt old guilt surfacing as the two of them approached the truck.

"Hey, Steve," Gilles greeted the passenger side first, with a familiarity that no longer bothered Simone. "How you doing?"

"I'm fine. Just had a good hike." He was making small talk, giving Simone time to figure out what to say.

"What the hell are you guys up to?" was still the only thought she could manage. Gilles and Jocelyne, at Ellie's house, made no sense, whichever way you looked at it. Gilles's nonchalant and cheerful demeanor did not suggest a crisis, but her mind ran on familiar tracks and she had to ask: "Something wrong? Mattie?"

"No, no, he's fine." Jocelyne had appeared at her window, also smiling and relaxed. "It's a giant conspiracy," she said. "Serge told us you would be here, and Ellie said to make ourselves at home. We've got something for you."

Ignoring that last bit, and wrestling with the thought that they had ruined her evening while simultaneously relieving her of the need to figure out what she had hoped that might be, she wondered whether hell was freezing over. Ellie and Gilles had studiously avoided contact for well over ten years. What the fuck was going on here?

"Steve," Gilles was doing a guy-to-guy thing at the other window. "We brought food. Stay and eat with us?"

Steve caught Simone's eye and a minute shake of her head.

"Best get going," he said, "but thanks."

He touched Simone's shoulder—the first physical contact they had made.

"I'll call you," he said. "I'll be at Dad's a couple more days."

And with that he fled to his truck, planting a kiss on Ivy's unmoving face. A whole day's hike had reduced her to the activity level of a piece of furniture.

Simone followed Gilles and Jocelyne into the house. They had found the wine and uncorked it, and had a potful of food on the stove. Simone begged for time to change and wash her hands, and came back to find bowls of chicken-something and full glasses of wine waiting on the table.

"Eat," Gilles instructed. "We'll talk after."

"After" came soon. With Ivy, full of food and groaning from the day's exertions, stretched out beside Simone on the pass-for-a-sofa futon that Ellie favored and Jocelyne and Gilles in the two comfortable chairs, Gilles produced a manila folder from a bag and slid it over the coffee table to Simone.

"Take a look," he said.

A folder of papers? Simone asked herself. What good is that going to do me? A new set of tires or a year's supply of dog food is what I need.

Nonetheless, curious and a little annoyed by all the mystery, Simone opened the folder. The first piece of paper was apparently a photocopy of some real estate information.

Four acres of cleared land on remote Patterson Pond in the Maine woods. Ideal hunting/fishing retreat. Small cabin and unimproved access road.

"What the...?" Simone had no idea what this was about. Were they trying to sell her real estate? Had they seen the state of her bank account lately?

"Keep going," Jocelyne urged, with a conspiratorial smile at Gilles.

"Fine," Simone said. She turned to the next document, this one in better condition and with a serious legal air to it.

Real Estate Deed, it read across the top of the page. This was followed by a lot of blah-blah-blah that Simone was too confused to read, but she could not miss the sight of her name, mysteriously appearing on a line labeled "Grantee."

"What?" she repeated. "I don't own property in Maine."

"Do now," Gilles said with relish. The dazed look on his daughter's face called for better explanation.

"It's a piece up on Patterson that I used to visit when the old boy was alive. He was sort of a hermit up there. It's been empty for years and the family never really tried to sell it."

That didn't explain enough, so he went on.

"I had to do something with the buy-out money they gave me." He had been paid to give up his university position under a program that bought off ageing faculty nearing retirement with lump-sum cash payments. This took overpaid, tenured professors off the payroll, to be replaced with newly minted PhDs, loaded with debt and easily exploited, who could be paid pathetic wages in the faint hope of eventual security. Gilles had jumped at the offer.

"The cabin is still there," he said. "It's a good log-built thing but needs work, and the road in is rough as hell. But it's a good bit of land, well drained at the top, and it goes all the way down to the pond."

That still didn't explain her name on the deed, and Simone waved it at him for an answer.

"It's yours," was all Gilles said. "I deeded it over to you. I don't need a second cabin, and you will know what to do with it."

Simone could only manage some garbled sounds.

"I, I…I. Uh, jeez," she mumbled.

"Don't worry about it. You deserve it. I'm proud of you."

Fuck, Simone thought. Hell has frozen over. She sagged against Ivy.

"Ivy, babe, we have a home," she whispered.

Ivy, whose response to any news was to lick the face of its bearer, stirred enough to send out a long tongue to collect delicious saltiness off Simone's face.

"Really? It's mine?" "All yours. Al, in Jackman, says he can fix up the road for you, enough to get in with a good four-wheel vehicle. Then it's up to you. Taxes aren't much and there's water in the brook. You could live there if you needed to."

Expressions of gratitude choked Simone. Serge broke the resulting silence with a prepared list of the goodies he had located in the Jackman spare-parts-for-cabins community. He had scoped out a good wood-stove, camp furniture, and recycled windows. Plus, he told her, if Al got in there with his backhoe he could dig her a new outhouse pit, and he had plans for the structure all ready to go.

Reeling under the truly weird conditions that this day had wrought, Simone eventually retired to bed. Yesterday, she had been anxiously waiting to see what a day with Steve would be like; she'd had no place to live and only a vague idea of her future, plus her neglected relationship with her father needed work. And now, by Jesus, look at it all. Kicking Ivy to the foot of her bed, she composed a text to Steve.

Today was great. Got even better. I have amazing news. See you tomorrow?? She wrote, then deleted, the last bit, as it seemed too pushy.

Seconds later the phone pinged. *Come over after lunch? Dad needs to meet Ivy and you can tell me your news.*

OK. See you then, she replied, and fell asleep thinking that sharing her news with Steve would be the best part of it all.

8

Two weeks later, Simone and Ivy were crossing through the Armstrong station for what seemed like the hundredth time that year. This time, however, the stop to check dog health papers was more complicated, as squashed onto the seat beside, but mostly under, Ivy was a small, underweight toffee-colored pit bull bitch.

Her hacked-off ears and the old scars that covered half her body told her story. She had been found, abandoned and bleeding, on the streets of New Bedford in Massachusetts, a discarded bait dog from some dog-fighting operation. Simone and Ivy had driven down to the Pit Crew Rescue of Massachusetts headquarters a week earlier, bent on a mission derived from hours of searching internet rescue sites. Simone had anticipated meeting resistance to her plan. The Crew adoption rules were strict. Home visits before a dog could be handed over; fenced yard for a dog; experienced new owners. Simone did not know whether a lonely boy all the way into Canada with an open yard and a single summer of pit-bull care under his belt would qualify—never mind pass the hurdles presented by her third-party adoption offer and the challenges that communicating with Mattie represented. She was armed with testimonials from the Saint-Georges vet and a phone full of photographs of Mattie and Ivy and the cozy home in Saint-Prosper. Her ace was an envelope containing a careful letter from Marie-Noëlle, backed up by a note from Mattie's therapist, describing her grandson's condition and the effect that Ivy had had on his survival of a devastating series of events. They would do anything to welcome a dog that could give him the support and companionship he'd had with Ivy.

Winning over Marie-Noëlle had been unsurprisingly easy. She had made Simone promise to find a smaller, quieter creature than Ivy, but his need for a dog was clear, and a rescued pit bull was the obvious choice. They could heal and help each other in a way that only they would understand, provided Simone could pick the right candidate.

For two days, camping out in a nearby KOA campground, she and Ivy simply took walks with assorted dogs from the rescue kennels. There were effusive ones, indifferent ones, and some that just wanted to play bumper cars with Ivy. On the third day, as their dedication to their mission became apparent, they were led to a cage in the quieter end of the kennel line. Pinned to the front of the kennel was a label that identified the occupant as PB 2 age 2 years, and a note from a family that had fostered her, carefully composed in a child's hand.

Please give Peanut Butter Pit Bull a good home. She has been scared a lot but she is very kind. She loves kittens and helped me raise six orphans. The author was identified as Charlie, age 8.

Another hand had written: *This sweetheart will be a wonderful friend for some lucky person. She is still a little nervous but has come such a long way in the month we have fostered her. She needs a quiet home and a sympathetic family. She is really very smart and has been a huge help to Charlie, who will miss her badly.*

When Ivy and Simone first approached the cage, the little dog stayed in her far corner and avoided eye contact. On their initial day out, she walked quietly beside Simone, showing no affect even when Ivy set off on a noisy exploration of the trash baskets in the small park they walked to. They returned her to her kennel and asked to take her out again the next day. She looks so desolate, Simone thought. She must be missing Charlie and the kittens. They walked again to the park. Simone found a bench to sit on, and as Ivy accosted strangers out at the farthest end of her leash, PB leaned against Simone's legs, pressing as hard as she could without falling over. Simone rubbed her head (how are you supposed to pet a dog with cropped ears? she asked herself. What barbarian would do that to a puppy?) and the dog swiveled her face around to look at Simone and allowed the tip of her tail to tremble.

"Oh, my God, you so need to come with us," Simone told her. "You are going to have the best life a dog can have. You are going to help someone who needs you."

She strategized her approach as they walked back. She knew the Pit Crew, a street-tough bunch of hairy, tattooed people who lived to rescue the never-ending population of abandoned and abused pit bulls from the streets, had taken a liking to her—or, at least, to Ivy. She would let Ivy do most of the talking, she decided. She would be the best argument that this was a good pit bull family. Then she would present all her evidence, and would plead for Mattie and for the little pit.

Some hard work and fast talking had followed, and now, here they were, having made elaborate promises that included future regular video chats with the Crew.

"I have a camp in Maine," she told them, loving the way that sounded. "You can come up and get a bit of woods life on you, and we can go check out how this little girl is doing."

Ivy had complained loudly when told to share the shotgun seat, and Simone had stuffed a bed into the foot well of the truck and pushed her down onto it.

"Suck it up, you spoiled brat. This won't kill you," Simone told her. "Just be glad no one cut your ears off." But the grunting and sighing got worse, and Simone relented and let them try sharing the seat again. After some negotiating, they settled on the double stack arrangement and the long drive back to Maine had passed without trouble.

It was leaf-peeper time now, the color in the trees strengthening as they moved north. The peak foliage season starts in the north and moves slowly south with the oncoming end of fall, and a wave of locals and out-of-staters was out in search of the perfect photograph. Traffic slowed with every view of brilliant color. The trouble with living in the oldest, whitest state in the union, she recognized, was that there were too many old, white people clogging up the roads in giant vehicles they could barely drive. The little roadside businesses were eager to separate money from this wave of visitors, and signs for blueberry pie, warm cider, and all day breakfasts were evident in every small town they drove through.

Simone was impatient to get to Jackman. As far as she knew, Steve was already there, and Gilles would be involving him in junk-pile searches for cabin accoutrements.

"We need to get there before they start thinking this is their project," she told Ivy.

It was evening when they made it into Jackman. The parking lot at the Moose Crossing was full, and Simone was glad to give it a pass. We don't need to prove anything to those idiots either, she figured. They are their own problem and welcome to it. The evening at Gilles's had been weird but not bad. She had pleaded road-weariness and climbed into the loft, leaving Steve and Gilles to bend each other's ears. The next day, they had driven, and then walked, up the rough track to the Patterson Pond property. It was as advertised, a good piece of land, south facing and sloping to the alder-ringed pond. The old field was a mass of color, the purple, blue, and pink New England asters now in full bloom and mixing with the last, late golden rods and Queen-Anne's lace. The cabin was better than Simone had hoped. A simple one room camp, but expertly built of hand-sawed logs and sitting high on stout boulders. A person could be comfortable here, she thought, at least for as long as it would take to turn the little camp into a proper dwelling.

But that would all have to wait, she told her father. She had stuff to do, first in Saint-Prosper and then back in Liberty. She would find a job in Belfast and pursue the plan to become a game warden. Ellie would gladly give her a place to live if she would stack wood and pull weeds.

"I'm serious," she told him. "That's what I am going to be."

Now, as she approached Saint-Prosper, Simone hoped that she had not made a terrible mistake. She didn't know whether Mattie would take to the little dog tucked under Ivy. She knew she could count on support from Serge and Marie-Noëlle, but what if Ivy was the only dog who could reach into Mattie's world?

The three Thibodeaus were finishing supper when she pushed open the door and let Ivy bounce into the room. They were expecting her, and Mattie was ready to fend off her exuberant reunion with the best of her besties.

When the greetings died down, Mattie looked up to see Simone and PB2 standing sheepishly on the doormat.

"Look who I found for you," Simone said. "She needs a safe place to live and I promised her you would look after her."

Mattie stood motionless, Ivy having diverted her attention to Marie-Noëlle's activities with the dinner plates. After a long pause he asked, "What's her name?"

"She hasn't really got one," Simone explained. "She was Peanut Butter Pit Bull for some reason, at her foster home. The rescue guys shortened it to PB2, or PB Squared, or whatever, but she needs better than that."

"What happened to her ears?" was his next question.

Oh dear, thought Simone. This isn't going so well.

"Someone cut them off. It's so there's nothing for fighting dogs to get hold of. She was used to bait fighters—they let them tear her to pieces for practice. But she is really sweet," she added on a hopeful note.

Ivy had taken up her station on the sofa, and Mattie joined her on his end. Simone unclipped PB's leash and waited to see what would happen. She cautiously approached Ivy, now her friend and comforter, who wagged her tail in welcome but made no move to make room for one more on the sofa. Pressing her case, PB hopped up anyway, and finding no room on Ivy's end appeared to make a decision and slid her body against Mattie. With a shy wriggle, she positioned her head on his leg and relaxed.

Holy pit bull to the power of two, Simone was thinking. She's a genius. She knows exactly what's up here. It made her wonder what Charlie had been like. Another oddball kid like Mattie, she was willing to bet, and the little dog recognized a familiar niche. She slipped her phone surreptitiously out of her pocket and snapped a quick photo. Charlie would need to know that his Peanut Butter foster pup had found a safe home.

Mattie's hand had found a resting place on the bony butt of his new friend.

"Could I just call her Phoebe?" he asked. "It sounds kind of the same so she won't have to get used to a new name."

"Sounds good to me," she said, as she felt Serge's arm come around her in a tight, grateful hug. She gave his hand a squeeze, fearful that any loud endorsement of Mattie's acceptance of the dog would disrupt the fragile moment. But it looked like she did not need to worry. Mattie had a real smile on his face as he addressed Ivy.

"You have to make room," he told her. "Phoebe is going to need some space on the sofa."

Simone pulled Ivy off the sofa and went to join Serge and Marie-Noëlle at the table, taking a cup for a share of the evening mint tea that Marie-Noëlle liked to brew.

"You going to be okay?" Serge asked his niece. "It's been a tough summer for all of us."

"I am," she was able to assure him. "It hasn't been all bad. And you two have been the best."

She felt she owed them a glimpse of her plans for the future, and found herself describing the day on Frye Mountain and her exploration of the path to game-wardenhood.

"You know that we think you can do anything, right?" Marie-Noëlle told her. "And you will always have place here."

"I know. And I can still come and help you in the *Érablière*," she said. "Are you...?" she wasn't sure what question she wanted to ask, but the future of Serge's business was on her mind.

"Don't worry about that," Serge was quick to reply. "I'm going to find a way to give the business to Mattie. He knows everything there is to know about making syrup, and is happiest when he is out there. It will take a few years and he will need a partner, but I believe we can make it happen. Maybe Gilles will come back and help us a little. There's a lot of hope left."

We will all find our way if we stay close to the woods, Simone thought. It was the best life she could imagine, and, as Serge said, there was a lot of reason to hope.

Acknowlegments

This book was written with help and advice from many extraordinary people. Friends read the story as it grew. They offered encouragement and kept me honest. Experts—some of whom I had never met before—gave me their time and allowed me to pick their brains for important details. Others let me use their artistic talents. To all of them, I offer my sincere thanks. This would not have been possible without them.

If I got anything right, it is because of these people. Errors are all mine.

So thank you: Debe Averill, Claire Bolduc, Barb and John Caron, Hannah Cyrus, Linda Dougherty, Mike Edes, Jim Fahey, Jake Galle, Katy Green, Lu Guthrie, John Herold, Richard May, Steve McCausland, Claire McKnight, Kim Morris, Kate Newkirk, Tom Pelletier, Johnny Sanchez, Hannah Peterson, John Welton, Linda Whitmore-Smithers.

And finally, thanks to the good people at The Writer's Colony at Dairy Hollow and at Maine Authors Publishing, who treated me like a real writer. It has been so much fun.